Also, By Tequila Barksdale
Tears of a Masterpiece

Ignite the Blue Rose

Tequila Barksdale

First Edition: January 2023

Ignite the Blue Rose/Tequila Barksdale

ISBN: 978-1-943616-52-7

Cover Art by Tequila Barksdale

Edited by Candice Washington

Publisher: MAWMedia Group, LLC
Los Angeles | Reno | Nashville

DEDICATED
to my dad David, my superhero and inspiration.

Nephew

I remember the last time we spoke just as if it were yesterday,
Your smile, your grace still lives presently in my heart today.
I think of all the memories that I have with you,
Longing for more, even just a few.
My heart will never feel the same
For there is a bruise in the spot that was designated for you.
I miss seeing your face,
That beautiful dimple when you smile,
Your laughter, not to mention your colorful style.
I never got to say goodbye and that hurts me to the core.
But with every twinkle in the sky,
I know you're by my side.
So, now I say to you rest forevermore,
As I continue to cherish each memory of you.
In loving Memory of Juwan

The Friends

Yazmine Bennett (Yaz)
Shynelle Raines (Shy)
Vanessa Housley

Table of Contents

Chapter 1: What a Morning

This has been a morning from hell. I woke up to a flat tire which made me late dropping Cameron off at school. As I walk in the door the lady at the front desk had the audacity to say in a stern voice "you're late." My initial reaction was "Bitch, I know" but instead, I decided against that plastered a smile on my face saying, "yeah it has been a crazy morning." Only to get to work finding out the head Chef has called out. Annoyed? Yes, that would be an accurate statement. I know that she is on another interview, but I wish she would have had the common decency to give me a heads up. Luckily, today is not a busy day. In the past year, I have had three chefs, all who have used my restaurant as a steppingstone to get to a more established restaurant. A master sommelier is what I need, yeah…the thought of that alone makes me laugh. I couldn't afford it even in my dreams. I just need that one Chef who can help elevate this place to the next level. Every time I interview someone for the position, they just don't seem to grasp the concept of what I aspire in my menu, you know a hint of the creole love my parents used in their dishes. The likeliness of that happening is slim to none but at least someone who puts some type of passion behind their chef coat to bring the magic out in my menu would be a great start. I just know if I could find that bomb chef, I would be able to attain that Michelin Star and it's on from there. Other than that, I truly have great staff. Most of who are young adults trying to better their lives.

As soon as I take a seat at my desk to review payroll, there is a knock at my door. It was one of the staff members letting me know that there is a rush, and they are short staff on the floor. Before I could call anyone in, someone from the kitchen staff came barging into my office to let me know that the assistant chef was in the kitchen freaking out because he has never had to work under so much pressure. As the young man closed my door "what the fuck" was the first thing out of my mouth. How in the hell am I supposed to run an establishment if I must be the cook, host, bartender, and now counselor? Again, I plaster a smile on my face, walk in the kitchen to give the chef a pep talk, then proceed to the floor giving everyone their roles for the day not to mention stepping in to get everyone caught up. Once I finished, I head to my office when I was stopped by Nyla, a college student, whose work ethic is impeccable. "Mrs. Bennet, you are the GOAT real talk, you do it all with class and elegance. I really love working with you. I have never had a boss help their staff at any job, so thank you." I smiled in response to Nyla, "We're a team, right? Thank you for coming in so close to the holiday. I really appreciate it."

I go in my office, close the door, and take a deep breath because I was feeling weak and overwhelmed. I finally make it back to my desk to review payroll when I noticed one of my employees who continues to "forget" to clock in has done it this entire week. I have discussed this with her two times. I know she isn't getting here on time which is why she does it. I guess she needs me to take further action. I really don't want to, but I must write her up at this point because she just doesn't seem take me seriously.

In preparation of the new year, I sent my excel spreadsheet and documentation to my girl and accountant Shynelle. She has helped me make several business and financial decisions that have guided me to get to this point in life. I sent her my documents earlier this week, but she only confirmed receipt of them via email. She normally would have called me by now to discuss everything. She could be busy at work with her new position, but it is still not like her to not call by now. I pick up my office phone and dial her cell but no answer, so I call her office. Her receptionist lets me know that she is in a meeting. I didn't bother leaving a message. I will just try to reach out again later.

I really miss my girls. I have called Shynelle and Vanessa two times yesterday and still no response. Shynelle and I have been best friends since we were five years old. Vanessa on the other hand, has been my friend since we were fifteen. The rest has been history; those are my girls. It appears they have forgotten about me since I moved away. In the past, I have always been the one to take internship out of the country or just travel, but for me to move, I must admit it has been an adjustment. However, not talking to my girls at least once a week is not cool, a simple text message or something. Maybe it is my fault. I put a lot on my plate when I moved out here especially since I was trying to open a restaurant in a place that was foreign to me. I have been living out here going on four years now and when I moved, we made the decision to come together once a year for either a vacation or gathering. The first year was a breeze, but the second year it was a little rocky. But we still managed to see it through. Last year we canceled all together and now it is almost the close of the year and no one has said a word. So, I had the bright idea to host a Christmas Party that seemed to backfire. So far, my girls have yet to confirm; now my husband has taken it upon himself to invite his coworkers, leaving me with yet another task to the long list of shit that I must do already. But that is beside the point. I am tired of reaching out to my girls only to be disregarded; even my brother Bryson hasn't responded, which is uncanny. It is not that I am upset with them. I just miss them. Now that Terrance has told everyone here, I guess I have no choice but to fulfill yet another obligation that I truly have no time for. That's what I get for opening my big mouth.

While sitting at my desk, there was another knock at my door. In anticipation of more mess to clean up, I take a deep breath before answering. To my surprise it was flowers being delivered from Terrance. My husband is my best friend for sure. He usually sends crazy things to make me laugh. So, for him to send flowers, I know there must be a twist. I open the card and it reads "These are just because flowers, so I hope to receive just because wink, wink- Love Terrance". It was just the laugh I needed. Since his career began elevating rapidly, our trips, date nights and just time together began to dwindle down slowly until one day it came to a complete halt. If it weren't for him, I would still be in California with my family and friends. But one day he came home asking if I would consider moving to Florida with him. He and I had been married almost two years but never had we discussed moving. I loved my home. I was doing extremely well plus my family and friends were there; I just didn't want to mess up a good thing. I also did not want to lose my husband, so I decided to follow him. Well, when he got here, he became even busier which made me step out to start something that I had as a goal for a very long time which resulted in me drowning myself opening a restaurant.

Prior to our move, I was one of the top commercial real-estate agents in my agency and I owned four single family homes that I still currently rent out. I didn't have any intentions of opening a restaurant at the time; however, when Terrance saw a space for sale, I completed my research and turned out to be a great investment for such a luxurious space. I had only been working for this small real-estate agency for about a month which wasn't the same feeling that I had back home, so I decided to take a break to open the restaurant. The restaurant was just not what we anticipated. Fortunately, I still had revenue from my rental properties and Terrance was well off in his career. By year two I was going to close but the market crashed, and we would have been in the hole in comparison to what we spent. After reviewing the numbers with Shy, we decided it would be best to keep it open for three more years then put it on the market if it was still not doing better. Well, we are ending year three and it still isn't as successful as it could be, but I must admit it is a better place than before.

After doing the noon walk through, I headed back to my office to eat lunch, my first meal of the day. For it to be two days before Christmas, it really is beautiful outside. It doesn't get too cold here but there is just enough breeze for a light jacket, in my opinion, to enjoy lunch outside. I might just go to the beach for lunch. As I was preparing the leave one of the staff members stopped me, "hey Yazmine, Cameron's school is on line one they have been trying to reach you on your cell." I replied as I walked back to my desk to take the call, "Oh shoot, I must have left it at home, thank you. Hello." The counselor replied, "Good Afternoon Mrs. Bennett, today is the last day of the camp and we closed twenty minutes ago! Cameron is the only person still waiting on his parent." I quickly replied to her discourteous remarks, "Oh, my sincerest apologies, I wasn't aware. I will get there very soon." The counselor continued with her rant, "Please, I have a flight to catch, thank you." It took everything in me not to call that rude camp counselor the bitch that she is. I hang up to call Terrance. He answers quickly as usual, "Hi love, what's up?" As I grabbed my things to head out my office door I responded, "Did you know that Cameron camp was only for a half a day today?" He quickly responded, "Yes, I thought I told you. Did you forget?" I wasn't sure if I forgot or if he didn't tell me, but I didn't want to take the blame for this one. So, I finally stopped thinking and replied. "You didn't tell me, but that's beside the point he is out, and his camp counselor is upset. Is there any way you could go get him?" "I can't right now. Baby, please go get him for me I promise I will make it up to you." There goes my lunch by the beach. I grab my lunch then head out to get Cameron. When I met Terrance, he had a son from his previous relationship. That was a deal breaker for me being that I was so young when we met. However somehow, he did exactly what he said he would which is make me fall in love with him. I have been in Cameron's life since he was two and now, he is twelve. He doesn't treat me like a stepmom, but he does know how to get away with things when it comes to me. When we were preparing to move out here, Cameron sat his mom, dad and myself down asking to move with us. Without hesitation I said yes. Having him here is that little piece of normalcy that I needed. But the pain in his mother face broke me in a different type of way. I took her out to lunch a little before we were moving which wasn't unusual since we have a close relationship. She cried but agreed that it would be best if he did live with his father being that he was approaching the teenage years. I made a promise to love on her son just as she would with her saying that she knew that I would made me feel okay with him moving with us. I never try to take his mother place, but she and his father made sure early on that he gave me the same respect that he gives them.

I finally make it to the school to pick up Cameron. Before I could say a word, Cameron immediately says, "Yaz, she was being a bitch, right?" I responded trying to maintain a serious look on my face, "Cameron, don't call that bitch, I mean that lady, a bitch." He smiled knowing exactly what he was doing as he continued to talk, "I knew you were thinking it that's why I said it for you." I had no intention of telling his father this time, but I wanted to see his reaction, so I replied to his slick comment. "I am going to tell your dad." He quickly responded as typical Cameron, "You won't. So how was your day? You look drained? I can cook tonight if you need some help. Ya boy kind of nice in the kitchen" I was starving but that didn't sound appeasing, so I hesitated in my response, "Really, what do you know how to cook, Cam?" Just as cheerful as his dad he responds with so much enthusiasm. "You know, the good stuff, noodles. What flavor you want beef or chicken? You look like a pork woman." We both started laughing. We talked all the way to the shoe store. Somehow, he got me to stop because I promised him some shoes if he made straight A's the first half of the school year. He is brilliant just like his father and just a little more fun like me, which is why our bond is unmatched.

As soon as we walked in the house Cam took off straight to his room, face glued to that phone as usual. I believe he was talking to some little girl by the way he was grinning. Now he is upstairs in his room playing some video game because I hear him yelling at whoever didn't catch his pass. The child loves basketball. I was already on my laptop finalizing things for work. I didn't have to go back because the second shift supervisor made it in right as I was leaving. She is good, so I trust her to close and not need much assistance. Although I was still working, it felt good to be home this early in the day. I hadn't seen a day off this early, hell all year. As I was sitting on the couch on my laptop I must have dozed off when Terrence walked in. He kept his word by walking in the house with dinner. Had he not, I was going to take Cam up on his offer for those noodles. He walked over giving me a kiss saying, "I didn't mean to wake you, you were looking so peaceful." It was obvious that I was tired, but I didn't want this to be a discussion, so I simply responded engaging in conversation with Terrance. "I needed to get up anyways, thanks for bringing home dinner." "Yeah, because Cam called me talking about what kind of noodles, I wanted so I definitely knew I needed to get dinner" (both laughing). Things were going great when he had to ask, "have you put anymore thought into taking a break for the new year? I really think you need it baby." This has been an ongoing discussion of ours for a year now which was becoming draining but to keep the peace I respond trying to change the subject. "I am trying to, but I think my head chef is on her way out and the assistant isn't ready for the position. Do you know this guy sat in my face during the interview and sold me so much experience but today had a meltdown under pressure, like really what the fuck?" "Yeah, I remember you did that shit for that internship in Dubai just so you could get there" laughing remembering exactly what he was talking about I responded, "I sure did, but I played it cool when I got there. I was trying to make college work for me. That was the last time I volunteered for shit." "I know, you complained the entire ride back from the airport, you never did listen to me not even then." I sat talking with Terrance for a while. We called Cameron down to eat with us as a family, something we haven't been able to do in a while. It felt good. After dinner, I was directed by the guys to go in the living room to chill.

Terrance poured me a glass of wine and Cameron turned on the television for me. Before I knew it, I was sleep.

Startled by the ring on my phone that I apparently left on the table, I quickly answer. "Sis, where have you been I have been calling you all day. Is everything alright?" It was my brother Mason calling to check in on me so I woke up to engage in a quick conversation with him. "What's up Mason, I forgot my phone at home. You could have called me at the restaurant you know." "Oh, I forgot, but I am glad everything is okay you had me worried. It is not like you to not answer when I call." Yeah, everything is fine I just had a crazy day, but everything is good." "Cool, cool. But hey I have a question." "Shoot." "So, you know how everyone has been upset with me for not going the traditional route of going to college. Well, I have finally finished culinary school and I was wondering if I could discuss a potential opportunity at your restaurant?" I understood Mason entirely. I didn't finish college and our parents blew a fuse but when real-estate worked out for me, they were a little more acceptant, but Mason got it even worse. Pondering on Mason's question, I haven't eaten any of his food in years. I mean when he was younger, he was always in the kitchen coming up with stuff but nothing restaurant worthy. I have been watching his latest YouTube videos and his meals do appear appetizing. "Sure Mason, when do you want to present your work?" Mason eagerly responded, "I was thinking this week when I come for the Christmas Party if that is cool." "So soon huh, but sure that works for me bro." "Best decision you have ever made (laughing). Thanks, Yaz I will talk to you soon sis.

Tell Terrance and Cam I said what's up for me." I have always held a soft spot for my youngest brother. I can't wait to see him, but I am not sure if he will be the saving grace that my restaurant needs, so I proceed to update my site with a few open positions, head chef as one.

Later that night when I was cleaning up, I received a text from Vanessa in our group thread that they have been blowing up all day. When I open it up the first thing I see is "Paging my Florida Boo, I know you are home; Terrance just told me you were there." Terrance walks in from the deck "Hey Baby, where is your phone? Vanessa is trying to reach you." I sit there laughing at the silly stuff they have been texting all day then I finally text back. Apparently, they have been trying to let me know why they will not be able to make it to the party or for Christmas, but I was just happy to be talking to them so everything else really didn't matter. Besides, I was exhausted just at the thought of hosting a big event made me cringe.

That night while everyone was sleeping, I was going over my year end expenses. I am not in the hole but if I don't make any changes, I will be this time next year as far as this restaurant goes. I am not sure what made me jump to do something so drastic when real-estate was going well. As I was doing the final review of payroll, Terrance walks into my office requesting that I come to bed. Terrance with many frustrations walks into my office, "It's three in the morning, Yazmine, you must stop doing this baby. Can't you see what it is doing to you?" I tiredly reply, "Terrance, I am fine. I was just getting ready to get in bed." "You're not fine, I don't know what else to do you just won't seem to listen to me." "Terrance…" before I could get anything out, he walks out of my office shaking his head in utter disgust. He really pisses me off sometimes with that.

The next morning as I was getting ready for work looking in the mirror, I just didn't recognize myself anymore. I have huge bags under my eyes that make up just doesn't seem to hide anymore. I barley have time to eat these days and my hair looks like it hasn't had any love in who knows how long. I got on the scale this morning and I was 105 pounds. A woman of my height 6 feet tall weighing 105 pounds is just not good. To make things worse as I was combing my hair a big chunk of it came out. I had to hurry to throw it out so that Terrance would not see it. Startled, I jumped as Terrance walked in the bathroom. "Yazmine, we really need to talk about what happened this morning. I can't have you getting two hours of sleep pretending that it is okay. As your husband, it is my job to know when my wife needs me to step in. Baby you really need to take some time off and refocus. Businesses come and go but I only have one of you which is why I need you to make some changes." In response to him barging in the bathroom on me, "You are right Terrance I have been thinking about closing for a week the top of the year to refocus and rebrand. Or maybe just sale and go back to real-estate" "You said this before, so when do you exactly plan to put actions behind those word?" "Soon, now please leave me alone." Terrance was right which bothered me because I don't know how I can close without everything completely falling apart. If I can get the restaurant up and running well, a chef that knows how to create art in the kitchen and staff that knows how to work could allow for me to have someone run the day to day, making time for me to work on me, sounds so simple. Or I can accept this as a loss and try again another time. I really must stop worrying about this right now; my head is already pounding, and I haven't even left the house. I was looking forward to seeing my family this morning. I was going to pick my parents and Mason up from the airport, but their flight was delayed so I guess I will head to the restaurant which is going to be interesting being that the head chef made it official by quitting. She didn't have the common decency to do it face to face nor put in a notice. She sent me a text at midnight. Hopefully, this day goes off without a hiccup.

Chapter 2: New Seat Please

As I was sitting finalizing a report to submit, Lisa barges into my office in immediate conversation as usual. "Shynelle, what time is your flight tonight?" "Hi Lisa, my flight is at 3 a.m. tomorrow morning, why what's up?" "My husband and I are going out for drinks later tonight and we wanted to invite you out." I kindly responded, "That's sweet of you two but I really have a lot to get done; thanks for the offer." "Well, I kind of actually said you would be there; my husband coworker is joining us, and we thought you two would hit it off well. Before you ask, no we are not trying to hook you up we just thought it would be fun to get you out a little more since you are still new to the city. His name is Nathan, he is a cardiovascular surgeon, and did I mention drop dead gorgeous. But he isn't one of those stick in the mud; he really knows how to have a good time." "Lisa, you have gotten me out almost every weekend for the past month and I am not trying to be hooked up with anyone right now." "True, so see you at the taco spot up the street for drinks at seven?" "Whatever fine, I will be there. I have to go to the gym after work, finish packing, shower and then I will meet you all there." Listing my list of things to do in hopes that she would sympathize and reschedule (wishful thinking). "Perfect, wear something sexy to show off this bomb figure that you have been working so hard on. You really look good girl; I can't believe you made such a drastic change within these past six months. Oh, and my husband also thanks you for getting me back into fitness cause this ass has been looking really good in these jeans lately!" We both laugh as she was nearing my office door. "You are crazy but close my door so I can finish up my work." "Okay, but for real look at this ass; it looks good don't you think?" She is crazy in a way that reminds me of Yazmine which is why she and I clicked instantly when I moved out here.

I never knew that my love for math would lead me to running an accounting firm. I have passed on the opportunity for promotions two times in the past, so the company stopped offering them to me. But one day I went into the director office and asked if there were any new opportunities within the company and to my surprise, she discussed the opening of a new firm in Arizona in need of a Director. I wasn't looking for that kind of jump, but I decided what the hell do I have to lose; so, I decided to take a leap of faith and it has been the best decision that I have made in my entire career. When Yazmine moved away almost four years ago, things were different. She was more than my best friend, we were sisters. I mean we have lived around one another since we were five so when she told me she was moving I was beyond hurt, but I could never tell her that. But after a few years I watched my friend step away from a stable career to open her parents dream business and I was proud of her. Her willingness to try something new with the uncertainty of the outcome for someone else was inspiring. That's when I started to reevaluate my life, pondering on what I wanted out of it. At one point I had become complacent at being in the background not wanting to be seen producing some of the best work. It was time for a change; it was time to believe in myself as much as I have believed in other people. I must admit this move has been the best, it has transformed me into the woman that I could have always been.

As I leave the office, I hurry up so that I can get to the gym on time. I hope I can get out of here without running into Mr. Thomas. He is the sweetest older gentleman that I have ever met but I really don't have time for one of his stories today. I haven't seen him yet so I should be fine. As soon as I reached the exit door, I hear a soft crackly voice "You are getting out of here early this Friday; I can't believe it." "Hi Mr. Thomas, yes I have a busy weekend ahead of me." "Okay, sweetheart you be safe and enjoy your weekend you know with it being the holiday season. Oh, and thank you for the early Christmas gift that you gave to me and my wife; we truly love it." "You are quite welcome and please tell Mrs. Thomas I said hello. You two have a Merry Christmas and Happy New Year." He and his wife own the cleaning company that cleans our building. They still come out sometimes to take shifts just to get out of the house. They are the sweetest people and the cutest couple I have ever met. They have been married over thirty years and although they may have had hard times, you can still see their love and passion for one another. This year was my first time ever being away from home for Thanksgiving due to work being so hectic. I wasn't able to take off, so they invited me over for Thanksgiving dinner. I felt so welcomed as if I were home.

Gym was everything that I needed in preparation of this upcoming weekend and the mouthwatering food that I have every intention of indulging in without shame. I had a great workout, but I wish I didn't have to do those extra sets. I was ten minutes late because I helped Mr. Thomas unload his cleaning supply out of his truck when he began to tell me a Christmas story back when his daughter and nephew were kids. I heard a little of it because I was really trying to be on time. Welp, my trainer does not play when it comes to tardiness so when I walked through the door fifteen minutes late; the smile on her face expressed her joy of the extra sets that I would be doing today. I have never been much of the athlete but now I am in love with working out. I mean I go on hikes, bike rides, boxing and I even take swimming aerobics at my gym when I have time. It relaxes me and makes me feel good on the inside. Not to mention it has made me feel more confident than I ever have my entire life. Oh, shoot let me text Yazmine to let her know that I haven't had a chance to go over her books before I forget again.

I hate lying to Yazmine, which is why I had my assistant tell her I was busy. She is such a fast talker; she would get me to talking too much then before you know it, she will know everything ruining our surprise. After tomorrow all of this will be over, and things can go back to normal. Now what is bothering me is trying to figure out what Vanessa must talk to me about. She called a couple of days ago franticly saying that she needs my advice but would rather discuss it in person. It's not like her to communicate anything going on with her so it must be serious for her to want to talk about it.

I really hate that I said I would meet Lisa tonight. I have much more important things that I could be doing with my time such as preparing for tomorrow. I just know this set up is not going to work. Since I have been here, she has tried to set me up on three occasions all of which I have declined. I just don't have time for dating, I wouldn't even know how to be honest. But to get her off my case, I think it would be best if I go just so she can say I gave it a chance so she can finally put this to rest.

Later that evening as I was walking into the restaurant, I see Lisa waving me to join them at the bar. When I get to the table, I am introduced to Nathan. We had food, few drinks and great conversation. I must say Nathan is a cool guy but there was something about him that wasn't connecting with me. I did, however, give him my number in front of Lisa so that she could stop trying to play match maker. Whatever made her believe that I was lonely was beyond me. For the first time in my life, I am content with my life. I can't blame her though; most people think that because they are in a relationship that is what you aspire to have. Plus, she is always wanting to do couple activities so I guess in her mind, I would need a man. When I made it home, I was beyond exhausted, but I still needed to pack. When I finished packing, I jumped in the shower, put on my pjs, got some ice cream, and flopped in my bed to cut on the latest murder mystery show. By the time I finished my cookie-n-cream ice-cream the show was going off, so I decided to call it a night.

The next morning, which was only three hours later, I woke up just in time to throw on some sweats so that I could go to the airport. What was I thinking getting a flight this early in the morning? I have never been a morning person no matter how hard I have tried. Yazmine freakishly is a morning person; I bet she is up right now working on something. I just do not understand it. Well, at least in a couple of hours I will see Vanessa, that is if she makes her flight. I was going to call for a ride, but I was running behind, so I had to drive. I really wasn't trying to pay to park my car being that I plan on being out there for a week. I hadn't told anyone, but I was going to stay longer to hang with Yazmine to help her out at the restaurant. She has been saying things are not going well but I haven't been able to look at her books in a while, so I need to make sure she is really doing okay; even help her come up with ideas if she needs it. When I arrive at the airport, I find parking, get my things out of the car when I was approached by some strange guy. Luckily a family was walking up; they let me walk with them to the shuttle which was about ten steps away. I didn't trust them much either because for some reason they didn't have many bags for a family of five. I could have just been overthinking, but I was glad the shuttle pulled up quickly. When I got on the shuttle the driver was very friendly, so I sat up there close to her talking until I got to my drop-off location. I arrived just in time to check my bags, get through security check, and find my terminal. After searching for a seat for ten minutes, it was time for me to board my plane. I was glad to take a much-needed nap because this crack of dawn travel stuff is not just for me.

As I board the plane searching for my seat, I locate my row. No one is there yet so I may have it to myself. As I began settling in preparing for the nap that I was about to take someone tapped me on shoulder. "Miss, I am so sorry to bother you, but my husband and I were just married but unfortunately, we were not able to obtain seating together. I wanted to know if you wouldn't mind switching seats with me?" I really wanted to say no but they were so convincing plus her seat was closer to the front of the plane. I decided to take her up on the offer. When I got to my new seat it was even better due to it being the window seat. I got comfy in my seat as the remaining passengers were boarding. So far, I have a row to myself which I am quite pleased about. As I closed my eyelid for a short period, I hear someone putting bags in the overhead above my seat which meant having the row to myself was short lived. I had no intentions of opening my eyes to greet anyone nor have small talk but again I was tapped on the shoulder. When I opened my eyes, the woman sitting next to me acted as if she didn't tap me, so I closed my eyes again. About twenty minutes into the flight, I had been hit on the head with a toy car, kicked in the back, Cheetos in my hair and burping in my ear. I was extremely agitated that this woman could not control her son who was sitting directly behind me.

By the time the flight landed I had not had a wink of sleep, I am exhausted. At least I don't have to be tortured by the little monster on the previous flight. Pleased to be departing that flight, I happily helped the mother get her bags for her and her son. Sluggishly trying to find my way to the next boarding station, I notice the lady with her child following me. I hurried up in hopes of leaving them but every time I turned around, they were four steps behind. I wanted to stop at the food area just to see if it were a coincidence that there were behind me or if in fact, they were following me, but I didn't have time. Before I could begin to panic, I notice them branch of to the restroom right before I got to my boarding area. I head over to my area waiting for Vanessa because we have about an hour wait.

Chapter 3: Last Minute Affairs

"Have a good vacation Vanessa, Merry Christmas and Happy New Year." "Thank you, you too girl. Be sure to get out to do something fun." I love my job, but I have been anticipating this much needed break for the past three weeks. This is the first year that my boss decided to close the office early for the holidays. She must have had a good year because we had a blast at our holiday party where I was able to have fun with my scrubs more than usual. I love colors, fashion and just being different overall but here you must wear plain black boring scrubs. However, this week she let us be festive, so I pulled out all the stylish bright scrubs bringing the holiday spirit to this dry, but nice, place of work. I received so many compliments even from my boss who doesn't seem to like much at all, so I know I felt that I brought the morale up in this place. Today, I may have over done it just a bit with the accessories on my hat. Being that it hit one of my clients in the face, resulting in me taking it off, hoping that she didn't file a complaint. Luckily, she was one of my cool clients that I have had for the past couple of years, so she didn't say anything. This week was everything that I needed to get me hyped for the fun filled weekend I have planned.

I believe that I have cleaned enough teeth this year to get my mom everything she could ever want for Christmas, which isn't much since she never wants anything. I just hope she likes what I get her. I have just a few more gifts to pick up from the store; hopefully it does not take long. Instead of going on the spontaneous road trip last weekend, I should have finished the task that I needed to get done, shopping being one of them. I really need to work on my procrastination. Now I am stuck out here with all the last-minute people, stuck in a ridiculous amount of traffic regretting the fact that I didn't stop to get gas yesterday as my gut told me to. Now I am hoping that my ass is not going to be stuck on the side of the road somewhere looking dumb.

After barely making it to the gas station and the hassle of trying to find parking, I have finally made it to the mall with only an hour until I meet my mom. As I guessed it to be, hectic is an understatement for the number of shoppers in here. Luckily, I already ordered the things that I need so I can just go to the counter to pick them up. Or so I thought, when I walked into the store there was a line to the back of the store. Before thinking I blurted "how the hell is there a line for pick up?" I was thinking that I should have walked pass all those people standing in line to get my things as it stated that I could when placing the order, but I didn't want to start any chaos today. Besides, the line is moving quite swiftly. As I was standing in line, I see this young couple with their two children. I always wished that my mom had gotten married so that I could have had that growing up. The holidays for me have always included only my mother and me. However, she never shorted me on making each holiday memorable. I just remember coming back from the holiday's listening to other children talking about time with their family and I never had much to say. That is until I met my girls later in life, they welcomed my mom and I right into their family never to exclude us from any family events. It was a different experience but truly amazing.

 As I was walking out of the store, I hear a woman call my name. "Girl, are you doing the last-minute shopping too?" "I am. I keep saying I will do better each year but somehow, I get worse. I only go shopping early for my friend who lives out of town just so she doesn't get her things after Christmas which has been the case the past few years." My coworker and I both laugh as she gives me a hug then walks off, "Okay, I will let you get back to it, be careful in this holiday madness."

After we said our goodbyes, I somehow ended up in another store which led me to another store. Before I knew it, I had gone into four additional stores, ate at the food court and was just now leaving the mall. That is until I decided to stop at the ice-skating rink that is only around during this time of year. I called my mom to ask if she wanted to join me, but she was at the house cooking, so I decided to skate by myself since she insisted that I could. I had a blast; I met some cool new people who were in town from London. They were a ball of fun. Once, I ended my random skating adventure I hurried home to pack and have dinner with my mom who for some reason thought it would be a good idea to still have our dinner even though we have an early flight in the morning. Even as an adult I still pick my battles with her wisely so this one I just let her have but I think it's time and energy that she could have put towards something else like prepare for vacation. I guess it's a tradition she just didn't want to miss out on. I love to travel so that I can create new memories especially with my girls, so this trip is going to be one to remember.

When I arrive to my house, I walk into the aroma of some good southern soul food. My mom and I are from the south so good ole southern food is just a little piece of home that we brought to California with us. After I speak to my mom I attempt to pack when I received a text that said "I love you". It put a smile on my face because throughout my entire life, he is the first man that I believe who has ever said it. I send him a text back "I love you too". My last relationship was forever ago, and the most memorable piece taken from it is the pain. I got so engaged in our text that it led to a phone call taking me away from packing yet again. I decided that I will continue packing for my trip in the morning. I always get things done during crunch time; actually, I think I work better under pressure. But I refuse to let Shynelle be right by missing my flight in the morning as she said I should have begun packing the other day. She will be surprised when I am sitting at the airport waiting on her.

I finally ended my call, returning to the living room where my mom, who is spending the night, is now dressed in the cutest green pajamas with a Christmas hat, snuggled on the couch with a glass of wine buried in her phone. She is probably playing some game. That is all she does on that thing when she isn't busy. "Vanessa, it is about time you joined me. I thought I was going to have to come up there and make you get off the phone in your own house" "I am sorry mom; I didn't know it had been so long. Are those the pajamas you picked out this year?" "Yes, they are, yours are over there on the table" "I hope you got me a size thick." "I sure did, you have your mothers' ass." We both laughed as I grabbed my pajamas preparing to go change. When I returned, I joined her at the table for dinner. My mom cooked a small feast for the two of us, now happy that she did decide to cook. After dinner, we were trying to find a movie to watch but so lethargic from the meal, that within thirty minutes of it playing, we were both knocked out. I cannot remember what movie we decided on, but I am certain that neither of us got past the credits.

My alarm went off at 3 A.M. this morning so I dreadfully got out of bed to finishing packing. I sit in my closet for fifteen minutes. I despised early morning flights, but I wanted to meet Shynelle so that we arrive at the same time. I am going to miss this flight I just know it. My mom who knows everything came in my room with the best smelling cup of coffee that I so desperately needed. I don't know what was so special about it, but I got up with the most energy, finished packing and we headed to the airport. I must admit, I was ecstatic to have my mom traveling with me as we have never spent a holiday apart and I was not ready to start this year. When we arrived at the airport, we were just five minutes shy of making our flight. My mom who hates tardiness was giving me the blues, so I secretly cut my air pods on as she preached all the way to the first restaurant I saw. I sat looking over the menu as she continued going off on me as I tried to figure out what I was going to eat for breakfast. I sent Shy a text letting her know that I missed my flight and that my mom would be joining on this trip which I know wouldn't be a problem because they always want her around. When I look up my mom still had a pissed look on her face, so I continued to let my music play. Ten minutes had passed when I was going through my phone feeling a hard kick under the table. The server had been standing trying to take my order but in the mist of trying to ignore my mother I was ignoring her. I apologized profusely and gave her my order. "I knew your ass was ignoring me, I watched your sneaky ass cut that music on as we were walking away from the terminal." Wondering why she continued to run her mouth for so long if she knew I wasn't listening is baffling. "Mom, I apologize. Besides, that lady could have let us on the flight." "You shouldn't be late. Oh, please don't put it on the staff as the lady was just doing her job. It is not her fault you have to learn to be more proactive about getting things done timely." As I was reaching to cut my music back on because I felt yet another long lecture gearing up. (Ouch!) "And you better not cut that damn music back on again while I am talking to you." I think she tried to prove a point with that kick, so I took my headphones out, to be clear that I was listening.

Four mimosas later, it was time to head towards our terminal to catch our flight. The waitress gave us the third mimosa for free because like everyone else fell in love with my moms' personality, then the two of them sparked a conversation that kept her at our table. She was cool, so

I didn't mind. Besides once she told my mom she was going to study law, I knew we were going to be here for a while. The mimosas were delicious so I enjoyed them, that way I could take a good nap when we get on this flight. For some reason after we boarded the plane, I wasn't tired a bit, more so anxious. I tried not to let my nerves get the best of me, so I started to look for my next trip which really calmed my nerves. I was planning my next vacation to Bali with a few excursions that should be fun for an early spring trip.

When we made it to our next destination my mom and I were lucky enough to not have another layover, so we had to rush from one end of the airport to the other side. We made it there just in time to board the plane. The host at this airport is way more gracious. My mom and I sat together this flight which I am not sure was a good thing. She started questioning my life goals, like when I will get married and have her some grandchildren. I am twenty-nine so I guess I am a late bloomer being that she and I practically grew up together. What I wanted to know is why is she still not married, instead of focusing so much on me she should try living her life, but I could never ask that without her getting upset so I scurried around the topic asking, "did you tell Shy that you were coming?" "I didn't but she asked me several times to come, and I miss her and Yazmine, so I had to make this trip. I miss you all together. My babies just have left the nest." "Yeah, I haven't been alone like this since before we moved to California" "I know, I was so happy when you met those young ladies. Does your missing them have something to do with all of the crazy, adventurous

shenanigans that you have started back doing lately?" "Mom, please
don't start. I just have more time to do things that interest me." "Well
jumping out of an airplane is just crazy if you ask me." "I didn't ask…"
I saw my mother piercing the side of my face, so I didn't finish my
statement, but I was thinking it. I didn't ask her opinion, nor did I bring
this up, she did but is upset with my responses. "Well before you say
something that gets you slapped off this plane, keep this in mind. You
are getting older and it's time for you to start taking things a little more
serious. You have a great career, extremely smart, and have a lot to
offer. I just want to see you happy." As respectfully as I could I respond
to my mother, "I know mom, and I am happy. If I, have you, I am
good." "You…"   Before my mother could finish her statement, I
interrupt her by saying, "Mom, please let's not start that conversation
today, let's just enjoy our holiday vacation. Thank you for coming, I
truly am happy to have you with me." "Vanessa, I love you and you're
right, lets enjoy this trip."

Our flight was great, my mom and I laughed, reminisced just enjoying
each other's company. When we arrived at the hotel, I received a call,
but couldn't answer it because my mom was still with me, so I stepped
off to the side sending a text message back. When I looked over my
shoulder, I could see her peeping curiously trying to determine what I
was doing but I caught her putting my phone away pretending as if I
were getting something out of my bag. Luckily, she decided to get her
own room because keeping her and my business separate would be
laborious. Shortly after arriving to my room, I took a quick nap because

we were there a little earlier than expected. Once I woke up, I began feeling anxious again. I had made it to a point where I really am happy, but I know that if I don't do this tonight that I will destroy something that means so much to me. I was beginning to panic, my mind was racing, heart beating fast, completely overthinking. Once I made my decision, I took a shower so that I could be ready on time for our surprise. Looking at the time I had to move quickly because I only had thirty minutes and I believe Shynelle is going to come to my room to meet me. Once I put my last little touch of make up on there was a knock at my door.

Chapter 4: Sight Unseen

Well, after finally getting my phone to work I receive the text from Vanessa letting me know that she missed her flight, no surprise there. I bet she waited until the last minute to pack. She has always been a procrastinator, but it somehow works for her. This secret she must share with me has me anxious. I wonder what it is. Hopefully, she will let me know when we are at the hotel. I hope I can get some sleep on this next flight. While waiting on my flight, I felt a small tap on my shoulder. When I turned around it was the little boy and his mother. "Ma'am I want to apologize for hitting your chair on the last flight. I was just upset that we will not be home for Christmas to open my present." I look into the eyes of the little boy who gave the sincerest apology. How could I be upset with him. I lean down over and reply, "Oh no, I understand that feeling. Once when I was about your age my dad took me to visit my grandmother for Christmas and I was just as upset as you. But on Christmas morning at my grandmother's house, I had so many gifts from her and other family members. I was upset but, in a way, I had two Christmas because I had gifts when I returned home." His mother eagerly jumps into the conversation, "See Eric you should be grateful to spend time with your family. The little boy who now seems to be a little bit happier hugs his mom as she turns to me and says, "Ma'am I just wanted to apologize to you because I know that was frustrating. I had to stop at the restroom to give a talk." She winked as she walked away. Right before walking off the little boy Eric turned and gave me the biggest hug. "Merry Christmas". I felt bad for lying to that baby because my grandmother didn't have me anything but a pack of socks. I was pissed that year watching my cousins open their gifts, being that they resided there, while I sat there looking stupid. Now thinking about it, my actions resembled Eric's behavior for a short period because my dad would have taken my gifts from me when I made it home; therefore, my tantrum was short lived. One of my cousins, did however share with me and right before I left my grandmother gave me an envelope with a lot of cash because she said it was easier to take back home with me. It was twenty dollars but being that young I thought I was rich. Besides I had so much fun with my family I kind of forget to be mad that I did not have any gifts to open on Christmas day. As I got older, I learned that it is not about the gifts but more so the memories that you create with the ones you love but as a kid I had not grasped that concept, nor did I want to.

After sitting on a flight with a man who tried to use my shoulder as a head rest and another kid using the back of my chair as a punching bag, I was beyond ready to get off my flight. I tried to be understanding being that Eric explained why he was upset on the previous flight, but I wanted to say something, however I didn't. Had this happened to

Yazmine, she would have turned around to the mother saying something like "I know you see baby Rocky hitting my fucking chair." She knows how to advocate for herself, something I am learning to do. As I was waiting for my Uber, I called Yazmine just to make it seem as though nothing was up, but she was so busy that I do not believe she had time to expect anything. She hurried off the phone thinking that I just was calling to check in letting her know that I made it to my dad's house in California. Since I have time, I guess I will take a nap at the hotel which usually is hard being that I have a hard time sleeping in hotels. It is just the thought of sharing a bed that millions of people have had their butts on plus the staff partially clean those rooms or at least that is how I feel.

I have been here for about five hours and fully rested now; I may have not wanted to sleep in that hotel bed, but my body said differently because I was out by the time my head hit the pillow. Vanessa sent me a text and a very hilarious voicemail while I was sleep letting me know that she had checked in to her room 1108B. I don't feel like it, but I finally get up to change. It is almost time to surprise Yazmine. Terrance has been in on this surprise for a couple of months; for once he has done quite well because he usually can't keep anything from her. Yazmine's parents and younger brother Mason are already at her house because they had already made plans to come so we didn't want to upset her. So, we told them to continue with their plans. Her two older brothers couldn't make it, but Vanessa and I are here along with her twin brother Bryson, who is in on the surprise too. She is going to play it chill but underneath the façade will be excitement; she is going to be thrilled. After getting out the shower I noticed that I messed some of my curls, therefore I am forced to search for my curling iron to touch them up. I don't see how Yazmine loves having long hair, it is such a chore to me. I have had a short cut most of my life and it is so convenient. I put on my makeup, throw on my black ripped jeans, black short sleeve fitted turtleneck top, heels, and an oversized olive-green blazer. After I am completely dressed, I grab a small bag with a few things so that I can stay with Yazmine. I decide not to check out just in case she doesn't have any room for me but hopefully she does.

As I was finally getting closer to Vanessa's room, I see Bryson wearing some tan joggers with a matching hoodie. He must also have a room on this floor because he still has on his travel clothes. Anytime there is a function this guy is dressed to impress even if it's just family. He has been like that his entire life. I would watch him take his hand me downs from his older brothers making them look like something to mimic a piece out of a Magazine. I would have thought he would have been a fashion designer, but he is a real estate accountant. Our love for math was the one thing that made us click but also made us very competitive. I miss him, and glad to see him. As I was about to yell his name, I choke beginning to cough as I stumble into the lounge area where the ice machines are. There is no way I just witnessed Bryson kissing Vanessa! There goes a sight I wish was unseen. I felt so many emotions, first disgust because he is like my brother, I have also known him since five. Two, Vanessa is like my sister, so it is like I just witnessed my brother and sister kiss …straight weird. I sit there for a minute until I hear her close her door and Bryson walk off. I hear him nearing the lounge area as my heart is panting profusely. I duck over behind the coke vending machine trying not to be seen but it is hard trying to hide with the noise coming from the heels that I am wearing. Fortunately, he turns the corner right before he gets to where I am. I can finally breathe. Just as I catch my breath, I feel my phone ring, it's Yazmine. I just ignored her. I honestly wouldn't know what to say to her in this moment. Now, I see what the big secret is that Vanessa has been holding and I wish I didn't.

Shortly after I gather my thoughts as well as myself, I knock on Vanessa door. Still in shock that when she swings the door open jumps in my arm to hug me, I didn't give off my usual happy reaction which she peeped. With a veiled expression of curiosity, Vanessa blurts, "Damn, you mad that I missed the flight or something?" I had to respond quickly so that I didn't give off any suspicious behavior. I responded with the first thing that came to my mind. "Oh, no I was thinking if I cut off my curling irons or not. Hey girl I missed you." She hugs me back then walks over to grab her shoes as she continues to talk. "Oh, well, did you? And I missed you too." "Yeah, I think I did. Are you ready to head over to Yazmine house? Her mom just told me that she is running late at the restaurant but should be home shortly." "Yep, ready let's go." Vanessa then turns to me with a forgetful look on her face putting on her other shoe as she as she hurries to the door. "Oh shit, my mom is at the bar waiting on us let me tell her we are on the way." "Oh, Ms. Gyles decided to come after all. I can't wait to see her." "Girl, she can't wait to see you all either. She talks about you two all the time. Sometimes I think I am the friend and you two are her daughters." I smirk with pride as I say to Vanessa, "Jealous still?" She is very much a spoiled brat and I love to tease her about it. She responds "very much so" with a smile giving me another hug as w laugh preparing to meet her mom downstairs.

In the car I tried to make small talk for a minute, but I just really wanted her to tell me about her and Bryson, so I asked, "so what did you want to talk to me about?" "Girl, you know what, it's nothing major I think I was just overreacting. You know how I get sometimes but it was nothing." I knew that my friend was telling a bold face lie but how could I tell her what I just saw. Vanessa has been in two serious relationships and the last one really broke her heart; I never thought she would date again. So, for her to be dating Bryson she must have sincere feelings. I really don't know what to say or do this weekend; therefore, I will suppress the vision that I witnessed so that I may enjoy this time with my girls. Then out of nowhere an eerie feeling rushed through my body and so many thoughts crossed my mind. What if this ruins our relationship with one another. What if Yazmine finds out thinking that I knew which I do but no one else knows that I know. She will be upset with me for keeping a secret but technically I am not supposed to know. What if she gets so upset at Vanessa that she doesn't want anything else to do with her? I am frantic right now at how this all could play out. Luckily, Ms. Gyles sparks conversation as she usually does. She is the youngest of all parents, but she ensures to push us to our fullest potential which is one thing that I loved about her since day one. She may be young but being a mother is something she just does naturally besides being the best divorce attorney.

When we pull up at Yazmine house, Vanessa's behavior became quite abnormal. She began to become very reserved. She and Yazmine are the least bit reserved. I hope she doesn't go into her house acting like this; that will be a dead giveaway, so I engage in conversation with her to lighten the mood. "Girl, you know she is going to pretend like she isn't happy when she sees us you know?" "Girl, I know she is, but we all know underneath that tough exterior she is going to be jumping for joy. I'd be shocked if she showed it." "She is definitely not. I am ready to have some fun with my girls tonight. I know there is going to be lots of fun, laughter, good food and great conversation." "Yeah, let's go in to see if they need us to do anything." "Yazmine's mom has already done everything, that lady probably has it set up like we are at a venue. I just love going to her events. Yazmine is almost on her mom's level just not quite there yet though." "Better not tell her that though." We continue with our conversation as we walk up the driveway.

When we walk in the house, we are greeted by Mason who I haven't seen in about a year now. He is all grown up and just as handsome as his other brothers. We all hug greeting one another. We grew up having family holidays together, so this is nothing abnormal; it's just now harder being that Yazmine and I live out of town now. I am glad that we can come together; it has been a while since we have been able to do this. Times have changed but the love we have for one another knows no zip code. Shortly after arriving to Yazmine house Bryson walks in dapper as usual. He walks over gives his parents a hug, then me and when he got to Vanessa, he gave her a very extra-long one. He flirted with her but that wasn't unusual; he has done that since day one. Things were going very well, nothing seemed strange at all. I guess I was overthinking things as I always do. Two hours after being there Terrance decides to leave to get Yazmine who was supposed to have been here already. By this time, we all have had a few drinks, played some silly game Mason suggested yet it was very entertaining and nibbled on some appetizers. We were making the best of it even though the person we came for was a no show.

When Terrance left, I sat with Byron catching up with him being that we hadn't seen one another in quite some time now. I tried to make small talk, more so hinting trying to ask if he were dating but he completely talked over me when I did. That wasn't uncommon, Bryson doesn't really date but when he does, he is private unless he is serious about the girl. That made me think…what if he isn't serious about Vanessa which drives a wedge between Yazmine and Vanessa relationship? He has had one serious girlfriend that I can recall. He talked to Yazmine first of course, those two are the ideal picture of twins who are best friends. Then one day he sat us both down to talk about the young lady to get advice on what he should do. That skank, however, broke his heart which really made him become even more of a playboy but underneath that exterior he is a true gentleman at heart.

He idolizes his father, so I know that deep down he too wants to be a husband and have a family of his own one day. But what if that is not with Vanessa and she too is one of his playmates until he finds his happily ever after?

I did not have time to sit there worrying about the possibilities being that Terrance informed us to wait about twenty minutes then prepare to hide. So, me, Bryson, Vanessa, and Ms. Gyles did just that. Our car was now parked in the garage, I forgot what Terrance was going to tell her so that she doesn't go in there. I think we should have parked up the street like I suggested. No one ever listens to me. As we were preparing to hide, I could see the nerves hit Vanessa as if she had been hit by a train. Her face was beginning to display anxiety as she looked sick to the stomach. As Vanessa and I hid in the entryway closet I whisper, "are you okay Vanessa?" "Yeah, I am okay. Do you think someone that you love could ever forgive you for doing something so life changing and not tell them about it initially?" "I guess it depends on what it is. Is everything okay Vanessa?" "Yeah, I was just thinking." Vanessa begins to cry so I grab her in my arms. "We love you so whatever it is, everything will work out" "Shy, you have always been the glue to keep us all steady. I have missed having you nearby. I see you out there in Arizona living your best life. It sometimes makes me think, what if it was us holding you back? Why didn't we push you to do all of the things that you are doing now?" "You did, I just wasn't ready. No one ever does anything in life until they are ready." She never said what was bothering her but now I know it has to do with her relationship with Bryson. I just hope Yazmine is just as accepting. We hug again as we sit being as quiet as possible until we get the okay to come out.

Chapter 5: Magical Night

I should have listened to my husband by closing the restaurant today, but I am barely making it as is. Maybe I should have just kept my food truck; it was doing well. But no, my overzealous ass was thinking a line up the street meant my restaurant would develop a line out the door, which has not been the case. I had a phenomenal chef at the time, but she moved away, and I haven't been able to get anyone who comes even close to comparison of the star she was in the kitchen. The food at my restaurant is just not it but I can't afford to close it. I still have another year on the lease and to break it would cost a fortune. I had three of my waitresses call out tonight which meant I was on the floor the entire time. Fortunately, I am closing at five because I don't think I can take another minute of this place. I wanted to open this restaurant for a very long time, but this shit is hard. I am tired, and I find it baffling the fact that my parents and younger brother are in town, and I have only seen them an hour; this is just ridiculous. This is not the life that I imagined. On top of that one of the stoves just went out which means more money going out and not enough coming in. I just can't take any more bad news tonight. I am going to leave work and go spend time with my family. Besides tomorrow is the first day that I have had off all year, hence I am going to make the best of it. As I was packing my things to leave for what I anticipated as a spectacular night I hear a knock at my door. Hesitating on whether I wanted to pretend that I wasn't in here I decided to answer whoever was on the other side of my door. After a quick second I say, "come in." When the door swings open it is the head sous chef who immediately starts conversation. "Hey Yazmine, you got a minute?" "Sure, what's up?" "I want to thank you for the opportunity; I really hate doing this to you right before the holiday, but I have been offered a position at another, more established restaurant as the assistant chef. It's not the lead position but I think it will help me out more career wise. Being that this is a well-known restaurant. It was on the Food Network just a few months ago so I think it will help me out tremendously, you know. I hope you understand." I somehow managed to smile as I responded to the guy not only insulting my place of business while leaving me in an unfortunate position. "Congratulations, thank you for letting me know. So, is this your official two-week notice?" "Actually, tonight was my last night." I tried so hard to plaster a smile on my face as my now former chef walked out of my office. Exasperated with every hit that I have endured with opening this restaurant but what is making it all worse is that I have nothing to really show for why right now I am not home with the people who love me. It took everything in me not to throw the pen I was holding at him as he walked out of the door.

As I was doing my final walk through of the restaurant, I somehow made it to the bar which before I knew it, I was sitting there drinking a beverage that I had in my hand. Luckily, Terrance came before I could drink my second glass. "Hey baby, what's going on we have been waiting on you for over an hour." "Terrance I am tired I don't want to throw a party." "I know baby, I've already let everyone know. I honestly think you need to take some time off you really look drained." "I have invested so much of our money into this place I cannot afford to take off besides I have so many people quitting on me that soon I will be the only person in this place." "Yazmine, I got us no matter what, but I know this place is going to pick up soon I just think you need to take some time off to clear your mind and come up with a new strategy. But right now, I just want to get you home to relax and spend time with our family. And don't do anything when you get there all I need from you is a smile and laughter. Oh, and Cameron tried to wait for you, but he and his mother had to catch their flight. He said he will hit you up tomorrow". I smiled at my husband who is truly my rock as I lean over to kiss him. I shoot Cam a text in the car. With the hectic day that I had it slipped my mind that he was heading to visit his mom for winter break today. When we pull up at the house, Terrance had me park in the driveway being that my parents have parked their car in the garage. Parents always say to get your own house and do what you what want but truthfully, they boss you around no matter where you are. I don't mind it though; I would move my parents in if it were up to me. My brothers; however, hate it especially my oldest two; their wives hate it when she does it which I believe makes her do it even more. When I walk in the house, I walk straight to my room, take off my work clothes and jump in the shower. When I get out, I put my robe on to find something to wear. As I sat on bed thinking of what I was going to throw on I must have dozed off. I thought I was dreaming when I heard someone say. "Oh, shit you do sleep, well not today slut get up!" Trying profusely to open my eyes I finally get them open, slightly seeing Vanessa standing over me yelling. I put a sleepy smile on my face then she jumps in my bed hugging me. "When did you get here girl and why didn't you tell me you were coming?" "You are such a control freak just be happy that I am here because from the looks of it you need some excitement in your life." "You look good you have a glow about you. I am so happy to see you." I reach in and hug my friend a little longer than usual. I have really missed her, Shynelle too. They have always been those to confide in and now that we are all off living our own separate lives situations are different, but I am happy she is here now. "Come on your mom has made a meal for the royal court in there let's go indulge." She goes into my closet, finds me something to wear, and fixes my hair. I hadn't looked this nice in a while and all I had to do was sit there while she helped me out. Talking my ear off of course but I loved every minute of it.

When I walk into my living room, I seen my mom, dad, and Mason. But as I turned the corner, I threw my hands over my face tilting my head back with excitement while also trying to keep my tears in when I saw Bryson, Shynelle, and Ms. Gyles. It didn't work. "Yo sis I haven't seen you cry since you lost your championship game in high school. You were ugly then and you are ugly now so please stop." Bryson is such a jerk, but it really made me laugh. Although, that didn't stop me from grabbing the nearest spoon off the counter throwing it across the room hitting him in the arm. Everyone laughed as I went around the room hugging everyone. We sat, conversed, and caught up for a while then we finally ate dinner.

After dinner I was approached by Bryson, from the look on his face he has something serious to discuss. "Yaz I really have missed your big head self. You never come home to visit anymore Miss Restaurant Owner. I don't understand why you stop doing something you were good at to open a restaurant. You don't even like to cook." I laugh responding to my brother, "I miss you too. I once could not fathom the thought of not being joined at the hip with you but now we reside miles away from one another. And to your statement, you know mom has always wanted a family restaurant, but it seems as though once I purchased the place, she and pops all of sudden don't have the time or energy to commit to something so time consuming." He still had this look of concern in his eyes as he replied to me. "Yeah, I know, it has been strenuous for me not to check in on you. And I have been having this feeling that you are not alright out here, from what I gather just looking at you in this moment, sis you need to take a break. Besides, our parents never told any of us to open a restaurant, they just always talked about it growing up. And now that they don't want it just to let it go". I smile at Bryson because he is my twin brother who truly knows everything there is to know about me. He is partially right, although this started to create a family legacy, I have grown to like being able to provide a platform for young adults as they entry to the real world and I kind of like it which makes it so hard for me to just quit. I have never been a quitter. But I didn't want to make this all about me, so I respond to his last remarks. "Yeah, I do I just don't know how I am going to do that, but Terrance and I will figure something out." As he stands up to grab his drink, he finally relaxed our conversation with a smart remark, "Do that because no one has time for your ass to be having a heart attack or something with yo old ass. But all jokes aside, I love you sis, knowing why you truly work so hard is admirable, but you are not in this alone. We are not where we use to be you know. You are overexerting yourself so take a break before you are forced to take a break." He walks over to side of the deck as he stares out into the yard for a minute as I pondered on the things that he just brought up. I must have taken a bit too long to respond because he turned back to me bucking his eyes waiting for me to respond. "I hear you and you are right. I plan to do better. Can you believe that we will be thirty next year?" I try to transition the conversation as I have had a hard day and this conversation was beginning to annoy me just as much as the Chef quitting on me a few hours ago. Unlike Terrance, Bryson knows when I just need a break, so he just went ahead with a new conversation. "Yep, I can actually. I am ready to settle down and start a family of my own." I was a little thrown back by his statement not knowing what to say for a minute but not to get into an even more serious conversation

I just go the safe route. "Settle down? Where is my brother and what have you done with him?" "Right here all grown up." "All jokes aside I would be happy for you to settle down give me a sister-in-law that I like unlike those other brothers of mine. "You love them you only pretend not to ruffle moms' feathers. "Facts, she does not like to share her boys for some reason ha". We both were laughing as our conversation was interrupted when Shynelle comes out on the deck letting Bryson know that my dad is looking for him.

Walking out the door onto the deck, Shynelle is followed by Vanessa who has been acting weird ever since I came out of my room. I cannot quite put my finger on it, but something is going on with her. "Yo bro, you mean to tell me you're not flirting with my girl today. Sorry Vanessa, I think he will be off the market soon." With a big smile on my face, I say jokingly. As Shynelle and I scooted over to make room for Vanessa to sit with us she coincidently remembered she needed to return a call. "What's up with your girl, she has been acting jumpy all night ever since we came from my room? She isn't on that shit, is she?" I said jokingly. "But seriously she has been acting strange. Usually, she is my turn up buddy that talks mess right along with me, but you have surprisingly been the fun one. I love it on you, I knew your square ass had it in you." "Why do you keep saying it like I was just so bad" "No Shy, you are the sweetest, dopest chic that I have ever met but you know you didn't see that in yourself. And now that you are embracing it; it really reflects on you overall giving you this beautiful oar. I am here for it, loving it all baby don't take it as any type of criticism" "Well thank you but you look a mess." "Damn…see that is some shit Vanessa would say. But I know I am trying to get myself together." "Well hurry because you are not looking well one bit." "Oh, forget you, I don't look that damn bad." I knew that I did but hearing it from my family back-to-back is really making it real. "Well, I plan to stay for a while to help you out. From looking at you I know that you need it." Shy says as she continues to eye me up and down. "Well thank you, but damn you don't have to keep telling me how bad you think I look." "Sensitive now too?" We both sit there laughing catching up on life when Bryson bring his ass outside turning our conversation into a math competition between, he and Shy. It was everything because although they are grown as fuck, they are still competitive about everything just as they were as kids.

I went in the house leaving the two of them on the deck debating marginal cost, boring the hell out of me, so I decided to refill my glass of wine. I walked pass a mirror on my wall stopping to see what everyone has told me from my parents who said it in the nicest way possible to my brother and friends. I was beyond tired of everyone talking about my appearance that the next person that says something just might make me snap. I didn't want to accept the fact that I was really doing more harm to myself than good. I wake up with a migraine daily, I barely have time to eat, I am stressed beyond measures. The harsh truth behind everyone concerns really has gotten to me; I have every intention to speak with my husband later tonight after everyone leaves so that we can do something about this. I may just have to take this loss, reevaluate things even though I am not certain if that is truly what I desire. I am not sure, but my health and my husband mean more to me than this restaurant.

I was finally able to catch Vanessa who seemed to have calmed down from whatever was bothering her. Or the couple of drinks calmed her down, not sure but she was more like herself than before. We talked for about thirty minutes then my mom cut on some of her oldies getting everyone up to dance. It was a magical night that everyone made for me. I was having such a good time that I didn't have time to even worry about the fact that I no longer had a chef for my restaurant. I was just capturing each moment that I had with my loved ones which was beyond needed.

Laughter, love, and a sense of peace lived in my living room at this moment. As everyone was helping to clean, my dad mysteriously pulled out a deck of cards for a spades game that lasted for a few rounds. The shit talking was real. At the end of the game, my parents and Ms. Gyles left for the hotel.

My brother Bryson disappeared so I went back on the deck where Shy was still cleaning up the last few items that were left out there.

Chapter 6: Perfect Timing

I hear Yazmine creeping back on the deck as I continued to clean the little mess that was left. "Shynelle the pictures you have been sending me don't do you justice; you look absolutely stunning." "Thank you, girl I am trying. I think it is the only thing keeping me sane with the heavy workload. Working out has been my outlet." "Well, it is doing good for you girl. So, what ever happened to that setup that your bestie sprung on you?" "Girl she is not my bestie with your jealous self, but Nathan is not for me. I only gave him my number so Lisa could stop trying to play match maker." "True, but it is good you are actually giving someone a chance for a change with your scary ass." "ha-ha, look who is talking I don't know how Terrance finally got you to go on a date with him." "He is persistent than a mothafucka, but I love my hubby with his fine ass." "So where are you all staying? How long will you be in town and why didn't you stay here tramp?" "Breathe, well we all have a hotel up the street from here and you know I don't like staying in hotels, so I only got mine for today I already have my things in your other guest room since your parents aren't staying here. Oh, and they leave the day after Christmas since you only got that one day off, but I plan to stay a little longer to help you." "Okay, okay I can work with that. So, who is Vanessa dating because she is glowing like she is madly in love but the whore hasn't said a word?" "Umm…" "Shit, hold that thought let me go get those other bottles out Mason asked for twenty minutes ago." Perfect timing. I was so relieved to be interrupted because I didn't know what to say. It is not like Vanessa has told me that she is dating Bryson I only think that I saw her kissing him. Hell, Vanessa hasn't told me that she is dating anyone so who am I to assume that she is. This is just too much for me besides I am worried about Yazmine she has always been a thin person her entire life, but she looks frail and stressed out. She has always been the one to work extremely hard but not to the point to where she let her appearance go. She doesn't look bad, but she doesn't look like herself. I just don't know how to say it without making her feel sad because that is not how I mean it. I need to figure out what is going on with my friend.

As I was trying to hurry away before Yazmine could finish up with Mason, I walked swiftly towards the guest bedroom. Yazmine house was huge so I should be able to sneak away long enough so that she doesn't remember what we were talking about. In the room I sit there going through my phone when I get a text from Nathan saying "Hi there" I was about to send a response back letting him down as easy as possible when I heard whispering. I went closer to the door when I peeped out it was Bryson and Vanessa talking. I didn't want to ease drop… what am I saying yes, I did so I stood there listening to their conversation. "I do love you Bryson I just can afford to lose the only friends that I have over this. Think about it, what if we don't work out?" "Vanessa, I love you and I want to marry you. She is my sister; she doesn't control my life and yes, she may get mad, but she will get over it. I want to be with you. I wish you would have let me tell her six months ago." "Look I love you too, but I really can't do this anymore. I hope you find someone who makes you as happy as you have made me over these past six months." "Please don't do this to me, hell to us all over what my sister may think." "I'm sorry Bryson...I love you, but I can't do this anymore." I see Vanessa through the small crack walking off towards the bathroom crying as Bryson is standing there in disbelief. The guy that I have known almost my entire life, basically my brother, someone I view as the strongest person ever was standing there hurting. The only time I had ever seen him cry was when his father was battling cancer. Although he isn't crying, he still has that same pain in his face. Against my better judgement, I had to be there for him, so I walk out of the room. "Bryson is everything okay?" "Yeah, I'm just feeling these drinks that's all." I watch him walk off like the manly man that he is hurting because he lost the woman that he loves. I mean he said he wanted to marry her. I hate to say it, but Vanessa has a point. Yazmine has never wanted anyone especially us to date any of her brothers but for me that has never been an issue since we all grew up like siblings. Vanessa came into our life when we teenagers, so her brothers were young men and I hate to admit it, but they are very attractive. But Bryson has always shown an interest in Vanessa, but he respected his sister too much to do anything about it back then. When she got her heart broke a few years back, he was there for letting her know that she is a queen and deserves to be treated as such. Yazmine was okay with that because she knew her friend needed it. Bryson is obviously in love who is she to block his happiness; because he fell in love with her friend. I think it would be okay, we wouldn't have to pretend to like his girlfriend as we have done in the past.

Later that night, we were all sitting outside in front of the fire pit when Terrance came back from his store run. We decided to have more drinks when, Bryson who has clearly had one too many, suggest that we play truth or dare. I could see that this was about to be a shit show, so I tried to suggest something else, but he was adamant about playing. Yazmine was going to do whatever her big brother wanted, so we played. It started off good; we were having a good time until Vanessa picked truth. Why would she do that? Yazmine was in the mist of coming up with a question to ask when out of now where Bryson blurts out "is it true that you love me?" Sitting there thinking oh hell here we go but Yazmine just laughed thinking he was just drunk, so she proceeds to ask a question. Bryson again stops her, "no Vanessa tell the truth. Is it true that you love me?" I tried to get Mason to grab Bryson, but he pushes him off.

Bryson: "Why do you all want me to shut up? Because I fell in love with my sister's best friend? So, fucking what? Get off me"

Terrance: "Come on bro chill let's not do this tonight. You have clearly had a little too much to drink."

Bryson: "Yeah, yeah everyone here is just scared to step up to Yazmine. Since you have such particular opinions about me why don't you tell my sister how you called me few months ago angry that she doesn't listen to you and that you're worried about how she isn't taking care of herself. Yeah, let's talk about that, BRO!"

I see Terrance jump up so we all get between them stopping what could have been a terrible situation. Terrance walked in the house furious slamming the door behind him.

Yazmine: "Vanessa is what my drunk ass brother saying true? And Shynelle did you know? What kind of fucking friends are you?"

Vanessa: "I am so sorry, but I broke it off with him because your friendship means the world to me. And please don't be mad at Shynelle, she didn't know."

Bryson: "She saw me kiss you today with her nosey ass and she was listening too when you kicked me to the curb. Yeah, she knew."

Shynelle: "Bryson please just shut up you have done enough tonight. Yazmine I just found out today, but I dint know how to tell you and it really wasn't my place it's not like anyone came and told me what was going on. Besides I think they really love each other girl so what is the big deal?"

Yazmine: "the big deal is that all of you lying bastards can get the hell out of my house!"

I watch Yazmine still going off as she walks into the house who is clearly going through her own little issues. Not to make things worse I acted quickly, thinking that she just needs some time to cool down, so

Mason helps me get Bryson, then we all leave to go to the hotel. I hope everyone gets their stuff together because I didn't come here to spend my Christmas in a hotel.

Chapter 7: Spontaneous Adventure

Growing up as an only child moving around, Yazmine and Shynelle have been the most solid friendships that I have ever been able to maintain. When they both moved away, Bryson was a piece of them that felt normal, and Yazmine told him to check in on me. Somehow, I fell in love with him unintentionally, but I never acted on those feelings until six months ago. I have never known a man that can treat you like a queen, speak value into your existence, inspire your flaws and show up for you when you don't recognize that you need that extra attention. I love him but I don't want to lose my friend over this. It's my fault she told me from beginning not to get involved with any of her brothers and I crossed that line. Now I am sitting here in a hotel on Christmas morning having lost not only my friend but the man that I really think could have been the love of my life. Bryson called me this morning but because I didn't answer, he left a voicemail. He called to let me know that he would fall back and not to worry Yazmine would eventually come around. The pain in his voice combined with his strength to let me go to make me happy demonstrates yet another reason why I love him. I feel horrible at my behavior. I didn't want to but ensure that everyone enjoy their trip I decided to go home. My mom on the other hand demanded that I go over there and speak with Yazmine, but this fight was not hers, so I let her know that I was leaving. I gave her the option join me or stay here. Surprisingly no one travels on Christmas, so I was able to change my flight with ease and although my mother did not want to spend her holiday in the airport, she was right by my side. I was happy to have her there. On the flight home, I told her everything that had gone on. She claimed to have already known about my relationship with Bryson but wanted me to be an adult about it and tell her on my own. She also believes that Yazmine wouldn't mind it's just the way it was presented to her. I am not sure, she is stubborn, so I don't think there was no right way to tell her that I was dating her brother.

When we arrived home, I was feeling drained like I had worked a full shift. When I checked my phone, no one had reached out, so I didn't bother to let them know I had made it home. My mom decided to stay the night with me. The next morning she and I went out for breakfast. She was still trying to get me to reach out to my friends, but I just couldn't do it. I was so distraught that I had to come up with something, hoping that my mom would participate. "Mom, we still have a few days off let's do something fun." "Like what Vanessa?" "There is this new place about an hour away where you can swim with the dolphins. It is indoor and they also have a cool waterpark. I can book us a room now." "Fuck it, let's do it." I know my mom hates my adventures, but I really needed one now. I just really can't stand to think about things right now. As we finish up our breakfast we hop in the car because our bags are still in there. We decided that anything that we need to get we would stop to buy it. It's not like my mom to do anything spontaneous; therefore, I am going to make the best of this trip.

On the way there my mom drove listening to her oldies. We made a stop at the store to get swim suites because that really is the only thing that we needed but that didn't stop us from purchasing a few other things. When we finally made it, we checked into our room with 30 minutes to spare before our excursion. My mom tried to get out of it hinting that she would take great pictures of me, but I wanted her to be a part of this experience. When we arrived, we were greeted by two older gentleman who appeared to be my mother's age. They introduced themselves. Samuel, who was a pediatrician, and Melvin, who didn't share his occupation. Samuel took an immediate interest in my mother showing it by helping her put on her life jacket. Surprisingly she allowed him to assist her. Soon, the rest of the people they were there with joined them. Apparently, they were there for Melvin's 45th birthday who had a cute couple's trip. Samuel seems to be the only person who is not married. I guess when you're the only single one in your best friend group, you still show up. Much respect to him. My mom didn't want to be in a large group, so we had to leave for our lesson. As we were walking in, I could feel her pulling away, so I grabbed her tightly. When we got to the pool she just would not nudge as she refused to get in. Both the instructor and I were getting annoyed, that's when I decided to push her in. My mom freaked out upon entering the water but after she calmed her nerves, she really enjoyed herself. When we were leaving out, she was sending pictures to her friends. But just as we were walking out of the door to exit, we were approached by Samuel who invited us to join them for dinner tonight. Behind him, the group that he was with were all waving and shaking their heads for us to come. Before my mom could say no, I said yes.

When we got to the car, I couldn't even shut the door good when I heard her say, "I am not going, I do not know those people, who knows what they are trying to do." "Mom, they invited us to a restaurant." "I am not going, and neither are you." "No, he wants to see you mom, go he seems like a good guy. Besides, when is the last time you've been on a date." She never answered my question but later that evening when it was time for us to leave the room, she brought up us attending dinner with Samuel. I didn't say anything I just smiled. On our ride there she seemed a little nervous trying to fix herself up. "Mom, you look gorgeous" "Thank you, Vanessa. I just haven't been out in a while. I don't even remember how it is to date." "Just be yourself and have a good time. He already likes you." "Look at you trying to give dating advice. I want you to be happy with someone, Bryson if you truly love him. I just don't want you to be work crazed like me. I just felt I had to give you a better life being that I was a single mom not to mention very young doing it on my own. It was like I had something to prove." "I know mom, I am grown now so it is time for you to start putting yourself first for once." When we arrived at the restaurant, Samuel was such a gentleman. He was waiting at the door waiting for us with roses not just for my mother but me as well. That night my mother really enjoyed herself. She smiled the entire time. She and Samuel exchanged numbers and they talked all night. He lives in the city near us, but we didn't tell him that as we still need to determine what he is about but if it is a true match at least they will be close to one another. My mother has already said she doesn't have time for long distance relationships, she is too old for that. I liked him for her so far. He owns his own practice, has one daughter who is twenty-one in college and has been divorced for seven years.

Later that night, my mom talked on the phone until she fell asleep. It made me think of Bryson, the way we would stay on the phone all night knowing that we had to get up for work early in the morning. Shynelle called earlier today, but I missed her call neglecting to call her back. That's when it hit me that I really did not know what to say to her.

The next morning, we planned to attend the waterpark, but I wasn't in the mood for it, so we decided to cut this trip short. My mom drove us home as I stared out the window the entire ride. When we arrived at my house, my mom did not want to leave but I just wanted to be alone. I grabbed the nearest blanket cut on the tv and curled up on my couch until I dozed off. When I finally woke up after hours of sleeping, I woke up to still to no call or text from Yazmine and surprisingly Shynelle had not reached out again. Shynelle would usually call again several times. I don't know where to begin with Yazmine and I honestly do not know what to say to Shynelle. The two of them have a foundation that was built long before I came along so maybe I am dispensable. They have never made me feel that way but what if it took something such as this to take place to push me out of their lives. I just didn't want to think about this anymore, so I got dressed in preparation of a solo dinner.

The rest of my days off, I went skating again, to my co-workers New Year Eve Party, and took my mother out for a night out. Although, I wish I could have spent my time with my friends, I managed to keep myself busy enough that I really had not had too much time to think about things. I had concluded that it was over between Bryson and my friendships have been destroyed being that I hadn't spoken to anyone since that night. I am hurt by the outcome, but I must find a way to get over things.

The Monday morning after a long well-deserved vacation, I dreaded going back to work. When I got there, I had a full packed schedule that kept me busy. My mother called me that afternoon letting me know that she would not be making dinner because she has made plans with Samuel, who she has been spending a lot of time with. I was feeling a little neglected being that I couldn't call my friends up or hang out with them. I have other friends but nothing like the bond I have with my girls. After work, I decided to make a stop at the grocery store to get some food for the night. When I get there, I pick up more than I went in for which is typically how it goes. As I was heading down the bread aisle towards the register of all people, I see Bryson who is with a beautiful young lady. The two of them were standing in line preparing to check out. They were laughing about something I wasn't sure because I couldn't hear them. I backed up pretending to look for a specific kind of bread not to look crazy to the older lady who was on the aisle with me. Once I see them exit the store I finally head to the register. I felt sad knowing that it only took him a week to already be entertaining another woman. Maybe, he is just that playboy from when I met him. Either way, I know I have no right to be upset being that I am the one who told him it was over.

When I arrived home, I really needed to talk to someone which is rare because I usually bottle my emotions in. I tried calling my mom, but she didn't answer. She did, however, send a text letting me know she would check in on me after her date. I had to much going on so instead of sitting in the house, I went to the movies. By the time I left the theater, I was drained plus hungry. I grabbed a bite to eat then headed home for the night. Once I was in the house, I cut on the most boring show I could find so that I could go to sleep.

The next morning, I just was not having a good day. I woke up to an empty tank and the gas station was jammed pack. Upon my arrival to work, I had back-to-back clients and a boss who just woke up on the wrong side of the bed. I was beyond over this day. When I got off work, I must hadn't shut my door all the way resulting in my light being on causing my battery to die. My coworker graciously allowed her husband help to get it started but he told me that I need to get a new battery because mine would probably not work again in the morning. He was right I was told to get a new one when I got my car serviced last month. I hate being a procrastinator. I made it to the store just in time for the nice gentleman to put my new battery in my car. I grabbed a bite to eat and headed home. When I finally made it home after talking to my mom on the ride home as she was preparing for her afternoon run. She basically told me to call my friends, or she would be calling them. I had every intent to give them a call I just didn't know what to say when I did which has prolonged me thus far. As the night was whining down, I picked up my phone to call Yazmine. After holding it in my hand for about thirty minutes trying to figure out what I was going to say I received a call from an unfamiliar number. There are some phone calls you just wish you never answered, the type that takes you into a mental and physical state of feeling paralyzed.

Chapter 8: The Revamp

After I ruined everyone's Christmas by being a complete asshole to those who took time out of their busy schedule to spend time with me including my parents. I felt like an idiot. Even though it has been while since the incident, I still haven't reached out to anyone. I just don't know what to say. Terrance and I got into an explosive argument which resulted in he and I mastering the silent treatment. We haven't spoken to one another since our fight. On top of that the day after Christmas I went to the restaurant only to find out that there was a busted pipe that caused a tremendous amount of damage in the kitchen forcing me to close after all. As of now it is looking like a couple of months until we can reopen based on the walk through with the contractor. But the hardest part about closing the restaurant was telling Nyla, who let me know that she needed her job because she was using it to fund her education with her last semester approaching, as she cried her little heart out. I felt bad but there was nothing that I could do. I sat with her for hours helping her fill out applications; I even wrote her a stellar recommendation, but I let her know once I open back up, she would be the first person that I call. She hugged me as if I had done so much but

I felt like I hadn't done anything, which is how I have been feeling for the past few years. My hair has been falling out in chunks, losing weight, sleeping about three hours daily and now losing all the people I love all for a restaurant that hasn't done anything but cause me issues. I felt weak like I was about to fall out when I felt a firm pat on my back; I thought it was Terrance but when I turned around it was Mason with a big happy smile on his face. He has stayed with me since the holidays. "Sis, have you calmed down now?" I smile hugging my younger brother who always seems to be happy no matter what he is going through. He reminds me so much of myself very ambitious which is why he and I are so close; however, I just don't know when I lost my smile. "Yeah bro, what are you doing here? I thought you would have left me by now?" "No, you said I could show you my work, so I wasn't leaving until I did just that. I know we didn't discuss it, but do you think I could stay with you and Terrance a while? I can pitch in on bills, Terrance gave me the okay but told me to run it by you as well." "Of course, you may. But you do know that it will be a couple of months until the restaurant is back open" "Cool, cool. What's going on why is this restaurant not open?" "Yeah, about that I have to get some work done in the kitchen meaning it will be closed for a while, but you are still welcomed to stay until then." Hoping he decides to stay. "Oh, yeah that is cool maybe I can help you out with marketing the place you know you really don't have much out there. You know this is the era of social media and you aren't on any platform's sis, but I got you."

Mason and I stayed at the empty restaurant for hours coming up with marketing ideas; he even helped me come up with ideas of remodeling the restaurant; minor changes which I could afford now that I have received the budget from the damage in the kitchen. I figured why not go ahead and remodel while it is closed. He took it upon himself to create my business page which I have known for a while that I needed, I just never had time. When Mason and I made it home I looked to see if Terrance had come home but he hadn't made it in yet. I called him but he didn't answer which is something that he never does. I didn't press the issue, but my mom would be distraught to know that I haven't tried to repair the issues I have with my husband which is why I haven't told her. She has already been on my case about repairing things with my brother and friends. I know that I need to I just know what to say.

As I was cleaning preparing for the night, I came across a planner that listed all of ideas and goals that I had when I moved out here. One of the goals was to by my parents a house. Well, my brothers and I brought this one into fruition about three years ago collectively. One of the proudest moments of my life. As I continued to read the things that I wanted they were mostly what I wanted to do for other people, in fact there really wasn't anything that I had listed for myself. Thinking about it, I have never thought of what I really wanted which is bothersome. I enjoy real-estate but I only did that because of my older brother. However, my love for flipping something old, busted and disgusting into something breath taking is something I have found to enjoy, which is what I did with my rental properties and to think about it, this restaurant. The best part of me opening this restaurant was taking this raggedy building and turning it into something nice, it's the revamp for me. I enjoyed every minute of it. To think about it, now that we are renovating, I haven't had any headaches, I have been calm and relaxed. Interrupting my thoughts by Terrance who came in the room giving off a basic, dry hello. I put my planner away to talk to him, but he immediately jumps in the shower. Stubbornly I decide to ignore him as well.

After Terrance got dressed, he went to the kitchen to eat then watched the last half of the game with Mason before he came back in the room with me. When he walked in the room, I continued to ignore him as if he weren't in the room when he apologized "I'm sorry Yazmine. I didn't say anything to be hurtful I just wanted to help you. I am tired of this childish shit we are doing. I am sorry." "I am sorry too, Terrance. I have wanted to apologize but I was being stubborn as fuck, you know that is how all this shit started anyways. But you are right, I love you and I am sorry." We hug, talk it out for a while discussing how Cameron decided to stay with his mom finish out the school year because she seemed to be extremely sad with him leaving her. He called to tell me and although I wanted him to come home, I understood how she feels only spending time with him on short breaks. In the mist of catching up I received a call from Bryson. Terrance didn't give me the chance to decide if I wanted to answer or not because he immediately answered. They talked things out the day after the debacle of a mess that was created like mature adults do. When he handed me the phone,

I rolled my eyes as he walked out back towards the living room. "Damn, breathing like a whale" "Bryson, don't start" "Okay, okay don't hang up. Old age is making you sensitive I see. But hey I have given you your time to calm the fuck down so what's up we cool now?" "Yeah, we are. I was just annoyed that everyone was getting on me about my appearance on top of me being stressed as fuck." "I already know, you showed your ass that night too" "Did I or did you." "I was drunk you were just an ass regularly so that tops my bullshit" I missed laughing with him. "It takes an ass to know one." "Definitely (haha) but I just wanted to check in on you to make sure you were alright. I heard you are renovating and working with Mason now. He is geeked ole peanut head self." "Yeah, he is, and I am enjoying every minute of it." "Good, good, well that is greato hear. I am making my rounds to apologize. I will get to Shynelle tomorrow." "Good, I need to myself. Hey I…" "Don't even worry about it sis, she and I just weren't a match. I need someone who is going to love me no matter who tries to block it no matter who it is, no disrespect." "But…" "Please just let it go. I love you sis; I'll catch up with you tomorrow. You can start back hitting me up now I miss your corny, funny text all damn day." We both laughed as we ended our call, "Alright, bro be safe love you."

At the restaurant the following day, we met with the workers to go over the plans. Due to the flood in the kitchen, there was some internal damage which resulted in work needing to be done in the kitchen as well as the eating area. Luckily, I don't have to pay anything out of pocket. We have enough for the renovations plus new furniture. The designs were great. I managed to get through that meeting with a breeze. Following the meeting I have to meet with Mason who created a mouthwatering menu that I hope lives up to the description He rented a kitchen space not too far from here, so I didn't have to rush. I grabbed my things and began to walk to the place. On the way there, I was thinking of what I was going to say to my girls when I reached out to them today. I know I should have reached out by now, which is making it extremely harder to find the right words to say when I finally call today. Before I could get too indulged in coming up with the best words to mend our relationship, I arrived at the kitchen space. When I waked in I was greeted by Mason in his chef attire and a table set for two like a romantic dinner. When I made it to the table, Terrance was standing looking delicious with a dozen of roses. I didn't try to hide the fact that it made me blush. Terrance and Mason came up with the bright idea to make the food tasting a romantic dinner for two which is the sweetest gesture ever. After talking with Terrance for a short period Mason began his presentation and all I can say is he did his thing. I think because he is my brother, I tend to be a harder critic but no matter what he brought to the table, it raised the bar higher and higher. I was extremely pleased with his menu, presentation, and attention to detail all while demonstrating his passion in his work. He has what it takes to progress this restaurant to the next level. As Mason took our dessert plates to finish cleaning, Terrance had the best idea. "Why don't you let your brother have half ownership in the restaurant, hiring a manager to take on the day to day and you get back into flipping house?" It was like he created a game plan that was magical. I loved every bit of the idea. I wasn't sure if Mason wanted that being that he had his YouTube stuff, but I was going to bring the idea to him. I was going to get with Shynelle and my attorney to see if we could come up with something that would make sense as well beneficial to Mason's future.

We finally arrived home after we decided to take Mason out to celebrate the future success of the restaurant. We hadn't brought the idea of giving him ownership in the restaurant yet, but he was now officially the head chef. The night was filled with drinks, bowling, and tons of laughter. When I made it home, I got in the shower then I decided to give Vanessa call. When I reached for my phone, I had three missed calls from my father who I immediately called back frantic. When he answered I could hear in the tone of his voice that something was wrong, and I wasn't prepared for what he was had to say. He told me that Vanessa's mother had been hit on her afternoon run and the driver called for help. She was in the hospital but that is all that they know as of now. My heart stopped, filled with a pain that hurts you where no one can see. My heart was aching for the unknown of my best friend and her mother.

Chapter 9: Pepper Spray

As usual without knocking Lisa walks into my office immediately talking. "Shynelle we still on for the boxing class tonight?" "Yes, I will be ready after work." "Cool, I need to go because I've been wanting to slap a hoe." "Girl, get out of my office." Work has been hectic since I have been back, so I understand her frustration. I was going to insert myself in the misunderstanding between Yazmine and Vanessa but I have learned to protect my peace allowing them to figure this out, besides no one has reached out not to even see if I had made it home. I love my friends, but I have been the peacemaker for years and that has become draining. I love them but I have also learned to love myself, putting myself first which may make me seem selfish, but I think it is best at this time. Bryson called me the night we left Yazmine house yelling saying I should have told her, and Vanessa got smart with me at the hotel saying I should have said something. For once, I didn't allow them to make me their punching bag by firmly standing up for myself which threw them both for a loop. I hate to say it, but I felt good about it. Now that I am home, I can focus on me doing what is best for me.

Lisa and I had a great time at the boxing class, so we signed up for another one next week. Mr. and Mrs. Thomas invited me over for dinner tonight, but I called them asking if I could take them out instead. They eagerly took me up on the invite. I learned that their daughter passed away about five years ago and it was extremely hard on them, but you would never know. They were very close to her being that she was their only child. I gather that is why they have taken such a liking to me which is something that their family has continuously thanked me for. However, I would have treated them the same way had the circumstances been different. They are truly the sweetest people that I have ever met. To be honest, Mr. Thomas reminds me of my grandfather who passed away when I was a kid. When I made it to their home, they were already ready to go. We went to a Jamaican restaurant because Mrs. Thomas said that is what she was in the mood for. We really enjoyed ourselves, I was shocked when they both ordered drinks. I am glad that I could get them out the house for a little fun.

When I arrived home, I just wanted to sip a glass of wine and enjoy a bubble bath which is what I did. I filled my tub, lit some candles, and poured a glass of wine. Insanely, I decided to watch a movie on Netflix. Before I knew it, I dozed off for a short period. After finally getting out my bubble bath I decided to call it a night.

The next morning, I felt relaxed and prepared for the day. On my way out the house I made my morning smoothie. As I was walking to my car, I see someone standing near my car, so I pretend that I forgot something and head back towards my building. But I hear the person running up behind me. Trying to reach for my pepper spray I hear "Shynelle slow down it's just me Bryson" my heart was exploding out of my chest as I stopped turning around recognizing that it was Bryson. "You really need to start wearing contacts or at least wear your glasses all the time." "Man, I can't argue with you on that one I just saw a blurry image of a man near my car freaking me out. What are you doing here?" "I took an assignment out here for a few days which came at the perfect time." "Oh okay, why?" "I wanted to apologize to you face to face. You are my sister, like it or not, and the way I talked to you a while ago wasn't cool bruh. I am sorry. You, unlike my real sister, is easier to talk to. You know she thinks she has to be tough because she has all brothers. But anyways, I apologize Shynelle for trying to hurt you as much as I was hurting that night." I punch Bryson in the arm smiling "It's okay bro. I know you were upset but if you ever speak to me like that again I'm going to have to kick your ass as Yazmine would say." "Ha, yeah, I deserve that. Well, I didn't want to hold you up I just wanted to get that off my chest since you haven't been answering my calls. I'm glad to see you finally grew some balls standing up for yourself woman it's about damn time." "Thank you for the apology, Bryson now get out of my face before I kick you in yours." "But for real if you are free tonight me and my coworker are going out for dinner you should come if you have time. I leave tomorrow and it's the least I can do for ruining your trip." I took him up on that offer and I have every intention to order the most expensive meal on the menu. Bryson is a good guy and I understand why Vanessa fell for him. I really think the two of them would be perfect for one another. I am not sure why Vanessa is allowing Yazmine to mess up what they have; it may take her some time, but I am sure she would get over it.

When I arrived to work things were hectic, I knew I wouldn't get off in time to meet Bryson for dinner, so I sent him a text. I worked over today but I still made time to hit up the gym where I was met by a creepy older gentleman following me around like a little puppy. I was so annoyed that I didn't enjoy working out today. As I was leaving, I let the staff know about his behavior to find out that I was the third lady to complain on him. He appeared to be up there in age, I would say about seventy or older. He appears to be harmless, but I don't trust anyone these days. As I was walking to my car, I received a call from Bryson asking where I was. I let him know that I was heading home then he got off the phone. He is such a jerk; I mean why call me to ask where I am just to hang up in my face once I answer him. When I arrive home, I immediately jump in the shower because I just don't like showering in public places. As I was stepping out the shower I was startled by a knock at my door. I grab my towel, dry off and grab my robe. As I was tipping to look out the peep hole my phone vibrates with a text from Bryson letting me know to open the door. I open the door to Bryson holding a bag of food from the restaurant he went to tonight. "You know you have to get clearance from your front desk to get up here, so you know it had to be someone you knew knocking at your door or one of your ugly ass neighbors". "Or just your ugly ass". "Ha, well I thought I would bring dinner to you since you couldn't make it. Besides that, guy they had me teamed with was annoying as fuck, I had to ditch him. Do you know this chump tried to tag along with me over here? I'm like, my guy I can't just bring some random dude to my sister house I don't know you. He was still looking dumb founded, so I just left him there to figure it out." "Ha-ha you have not changed at all. I don't know how you have friends you are so mean just like Yazmine." Failing to realize that he may not be ready to talk about his sister just yet, but he didn't seem to be bothered. "No, now she is mean. You remember when those boys hit you with a kick ball and she got a sock of rocks walked over threating to beat them with it unless they apologized to you when we were kids?" "Ha, ha, yeah, she was crazy. When I asked her, what made her do it she said it was something she saw on a movie, and she hoped it worked because she didn't want to get in trouble for hitting them with those rocks". Bryson ended up staying the night because he didn't want to be met by his coworker at the hotel. We sat up talking while he watched the game until I got sleepy.

The next morning Bryson got up early so that he could catch his flight back home and I prepared to go to work. I received a call from Lisa letting me know that she will be returning to work today so not to worry about any of her work because she previously planned to take the day off. I was glad because I had extremely too much on my plate. On my way to work I receive a call from Yazmine who starts off by apologizing. She then began informing of what has happened to Ms. Gyles. We decided to make a visit which will allow Yazmine and

Vanessa to talk face to face. When I finally reached a stopping point at work, I found a ticket to leave out tonight.

Chapter 10: Fearless

After being scared out of my mind to see my mother and hold her made everything alright. The unknown of her condition really had me in a choke hold. My nerves had gotten the best of me. I didn't know what to do. I called Yazmine's parents who were there instantly because I was falling apart silently. My mother is all that I have and the thought of losing her put me in a state of being that I cannot explain. When Yazmine's parents made it to my house I was still pacing back and forward in my living room, grabbing clothes out of a basket as if I were folding them. I had the same shirt going in circles when Mrs. Paul grabbed me close, hugging me to calm down. They drove me to the hospital; when we pulled up, I didn't say a word. I just felt tears that I had been somehow holding in roll down my cheek. As we walked to the front desk, they took the lead because I wasn't in the right head space. We took a seat as they informed us that someone would be with us shortly. Those ten minutes felt like days, my knee was shaking so hard that Mrs. Paul again had to calm me down. When the doctor approached me, I grabbed her hand like a little kid seeking protection and she held mines like a parent who will always be a protector.

As we walked to my mothers' room, I felt a sigh of relief when I heard her say, "well, that was the craziest run I have ever been on" with the most beautiful smile on her face. She reached out to give me a hug. She was doing fine. "That kid was so busy trying to take a video that he hit me with his damn car, luckily, he was driving extremely slow that it didn't hit me at a high impact. I wanted to be mad at him, but he was crying and being very apologetic that I felt that it should be a teachable moment. Plus, he called for help before I could get a word in. His parent just left, and they were also apologetic but when they found out that I was a lawyer, the concern on their face hit an all-time high. I could tell the young man was going to get the business when he got home. We exchanged information and they have already agreed to pay any hospital expenses." "I am just glad you are okay mom" "Me too baby" We sat up there about an hour waiting to find out if they were going to release her from the hospital. She had one scratch on her elbow and cheek but seemed fine. They wanted to make sure she didn't suffer a internal issues before releasing her.

After about an hour she was released to go home. We were both dropped off at my place because I just didn't want her to be alone tonight. Mr. and Mrs. Paul left for home as my mother, and I prepared for the night. I ordered food while she showered. Although, my mom was fine the thought of losing her lingered on my mind. I was still a little shaken up by everything that happened today. I felt so alone. This situation made me really miss Shynelle and Vanessa. It made me think of my behavior realizing that if I just knew how to face my fears, communicate, and not procrastinate on doing things, then I probably wouldn't be in this predicament. I solely take accountability of my actions wishing that I just knew how to reach out to them. I never intended on things to become so arduous between us. Resulting in something this drastic to make me realize that me running away from my problems only create new ones that are sometimes harder to come back from. I watched my mom who I idolized and although she had her reasons for stepping out proving that she could do it alone, I don't want to. I am grateful that she has given me every tool to stand alone but that is not the life I desire for myself but if I don't start addressing things as they arise, that is exactly how I will be…alone. For the first time in a very long time, I sat listening to my mom talk, lecture and give pure valuable life information realizing that all this time she hasn't just been preparing me to be alone she has been preparing me to see life differently than she has. It took for her to have an accident to stop and listen to everything that she has been trying to tell me whereas I would only take the surface information then tune her out. Tonight, was different, tonight I learned more about my mom as well as myself.

I concluded that I needed to make things right or at least, attempt to. I could have approached this entire situation differently, probably resulting in a different outcome. I spoke to Shynelle reckless that night and she didn't deserve it, but top of that she still reached out. Yazmine was going through her own issues and me keeping this a secret from her probably just took her over the edge. I was so busy trying to find a way around confronting my issue that I didn't see my flaws within this entire situation making me feel worse for allowing so much time to pass. By the time I went to bed I decided that tomorrow I would put forth my best efforts to mend things with everyone.

Chapter 11: Flannel Pants

After finding out what happened to Ms. Gyles, I immediately purchased a ticket back home. I let Terrance know that he didn't have to go being that she was doing fine, and Mason would be accompanying me. He still tried but was not able to with his busy workload. When we made it to California, I became extremely nervous as to how Vanessa will welcome me being that I caused such a mess between everyone a while ago. I felt ashamed that I had not reached out sooner to mend things with my friends. Now that this has occurred, I am walking in disgusted by my behavior hoping that she accepts that I genuinely care. When we landed, I sent my things with Mason so that I could go straight to Vanessa and Ms. Gyles. My mom let me know that they were still at Vanessa's place as she had just dropped some food off for the two of them earlier. I hoped that Ms. Gyles is still there when I arrived to break some of the tension.

As I walk to Vanessa door, I hear music playing on the opposite side. I knock but I am not sure anyone heard me, so I knocked again this time a little harder. In less than a second of me knocking Vanessa was standing in front of me with a stunned look on her face. When it did not appear that she was going to invite me in; I hear Ms. Gyles who appeared to be preparing to leave request that I come in. "Hi Ms. Gyles, I am so pleased to see that you are doing okay." "Yes, baby I am fine. You did not have to come all the way across the world to check on me, I told you yesterday that I was doing just fine." "I know but I needed to see you in person I just had to." I gave her another big hug as she embraced me as she always does. "Well, I was just preparing to head home for a while, but you should stop by to see me for dinner tonight, I'd love that." "First, I would like to apologize to you for ruining your holidays I was just well no excuses I apologize. And I would love to join you for dinner." "I forgave you a month ago baby but thank you. I know you were just going through your own little situation, and it got the best of you. I understand and don't worry I still love you just the same." She smiled giving me another hug followed by a kiss on the cheek. "Now you two, kiss and make up. I will see you both tonight for dinner." She walked out before either of us could say a word. She was like that, every time we got into it with one another she pushed for us to work it out before she got involved because with her the long speeches were far worse than just working it out on our own.

"I'm sorry Vanessa for treating you the way I did. I..." "I am sorry for not telling you about Bryson and me. I was so torn between the thought of losing the only family that I have created or being happy with a man that I love. I love Bryson so much I do, but the thought of losing you and Shynelle really scared the hell out of me. When I got the news about my mom, I was so lost that she is the only person I have. If something were to happen to her, I'd be broken. I didn't have you all to call. I was embedded in a sea of pain and uncertainty feeling forced to face it on my own which has been one of my biggest fears of life." I hugged my friend as I wiped her tears from her eyes. "You never have to worry about being alone, nothing you can do will ever come between us to destroy the foundation that we have built, not even my big-headed brother." I could see a smile form on her face as she said, "Yaz, I appreciate you saying this to me. I have never had a family until I met you all. The way your parents came to be by my side yesterday, I just can never thank them enough." "That is was family is for girl." We sat talked for over an hour as if nothing had ever gone wrong between us. It was apparent that Vanessa needed us more than we thought, I was glad to hear that she wanted to work on herself as a person. I shared with her everything that happen since the last time we spoke. It was as if we were all going through a period of growth. I wasn't sure what mine was now but hell I hope that is what this mess I am in is. As we were sitting at the table catching up there was a knock at the door. I believed it to be Shynelle, but I wasn't sure if she had told Vanessa, so I didn't say anything. When Vanessa opened the door to my surprise it was Bryson. When she saw that it was him, I could see her look at me as if she were a kid who was seeking their parents' approval. "Look, I have always known you two would get together so I don't know why you tried to keep it a secret. I am fine with whatever you decide to do. I am sorry for messing what you two had going on seriously, I was just going through my own shit, and everyone was getting on my nerves as usual." Vanessa smiled in a way that she had never smiled before about a guy. Bryson smirked because well its Bryson. I wanted to stay to be nosey but I received a call from Cameron. We all talked shortly before I had to leave coming to the agreement that we forgive one another for our roles in the holiday blow up and that was the end of the conversation.

On my way to meet Cameron it lingered in my mind what was going to be the outcome of their conversation. He had just told me before Ms. Gyles accident that he wanted a woman who would fight for him regardless of the situation sounding pretty sure of himself. But the way he showed up for her today really showed me how much he cares for her. I have known him my entire life and he is not one to show a female his emotions so there must be something there. I guess I will have to find out later because I have every intention on asking. When I arrived for lunch, Cameron and his mother were already there. We talked catching up on everything Cameron. He apologized profusely for leaving his dad and I explained how he just could not leave his mother who he had really been missing. I didn't need an explanation, I understood that he needs her. He is now going to come spend time with us on holidays and stay with his mom throughout the year. After lunch, I received a message from Shy letting me know that she was in town, that she would see me later at Ms. Gyles for dinner.

Later that evening when we arrived for dinner it was me, my parents, Mason, Shynelle, Vanessa, Bryson, and Ms. Gyles new boo Dr. Samuels. I didn't have to ask if Vanessa and Bryson made up because the way they displayed their affection the entire evening. I must admit it was cute and not awkward at all being that they have always playfully flirted. I see Shynelle over by the table looking at the spread Ms. Gyles has prepared. "Looks good doesn't it" "It does, anticipating the moment she tells us she is ready because I am starving." "Here, take these crackers they may hold you over for a few minutes." She takes them, devouring them in two seconds. "So, how does it feel to see them all booed up?" "I was just thinking to myself it is not awkward at all coincidently." "It's not actually." "So, are you dating anyone that I should know about?" "Not even on my radar, I am so swamped with work that I don't really have much time to anything but work. I think I like it like that." "Well make time for it." "I don't see myself like you and Vanessa. Don't get me wrong I love it on you two, but I don't think that is for me." "I know, I just want to see you with the big goofy grin Vanessa has right now one day because you deserve it too." We both look over at Vanessa laughing because she had the biggest smile on her face as if she were posing for a picture. "She most definitely has been showing those big teeth off all night. I am happy for our girl though." "Me too" In the middle of our conversation, Ms. Gyles invited us all to come join at the table for dinner.

The night was going well. As we were sitting waiting for dessert Bryson threw a dinner roll hitting me in the eye. I am not sure why he is still so childish, but everyone thought it was funny. I didn't because my lash had fallen off so now, I was sitting there looking foolish. I tried to play it cool with every intention of getting him back. As we were getting up from the table, I tried to trip him, but the joke was on me when my pants split down the middle, now everyone seeing all my business. I was mortified but the kicker were the flannel pants that Ms. Gyles gave me to wear. She had a curvy body, so they were way too big resulting in me having to tie a belt around them to stay up, they were just hideous. Not to mention it didn't go with anything that I had on. So, now I was sitting in the living room wearing flannel pants, purple top with one eyelash. I didn't think it could get any worse when Bryson tagged me in a post. When I opened it up, there I was sitting on the couch looking ridiculous. Before I could do anything Terrance calls. Knowing exactly why he was calling I ignored him. I didn't let it get the best of me; in fact, I still enjoyed the rest of the night as if I were the most stylish person in the room. By the end of the night after the rain stopped, we all decided to go our separate ways. When I got halfway to the car, I hear a loud noise, when I turned around Bryson had fallen face forward in a big ass puddle making my night perfect. Sometimes the universe fights your battle and this one was won.

Chapter 12: Impulsive Decision

It had been a few weeks since the ladies had left, my mom was doing fine, and I am happy. I had a deep conversation with my mom about the feeling of it only being the two of us and how that has impacted me as an adult. She understood and suggested counseling. She even shared that she had gone for a while when I was younger. Shynelle asked me to go when she started but I didn't see why I would need it. Well, after she left, I called her up and we talked about her experience with it, deciding to give it a try. I have only been going a short period but learning to heal past trauma is something that I believe that I have needed. Processing how to work through my emotions rather than covering them with trips and adventures to avoid what I really needed to deal with was a big take away for me. I never put much between the two but after the therapist called it out, denying it of course but she is right. Although, I still have a passion for traveling I can't just take a random trip when I need to avoid real life shit, I guess it what the therapist has been trying to get me to learn. I continued to think about my session as I prepared to go home to pack in preparation of the weekend. Bryson had the bright idea for my mom, Samuel, and I to do a couple's weekend in Vegas. Surprisingly my mom was all for it, so I had to jump on board quickly before she changed her mind. This new guy has really brought out a side of her that I hadn't seen before. To think of it, I never saw my mom date anyone, so this is a first. He makes her happy; I am excited for her. After searching for my suitcase that I could never find, I settled for the smaller green one that I used on my previous trip. I go through my clothes recognizing that the only black pieces that I have are the scrubs that I wear to work. I just love the way bright colors make me feel, happy, just excited overall and joyful. However, I have turned it down some over the past few years; my love for fashion and color are two things that will just not change. I find a few pieces plus a few extra to get me through the weekend. I wouldn't say that I over pack, but I sure don't under pack. After finally getting my suitcase to close after wrestling with it for over ten minutes I was ready for this weekend.

When Bryson arrives, he is already ready to go. He and his sister are most definitely twins, because they are the most punctual individuals I know. "I bet you haven't packed yet, have you?" "I most certainly did not!" Just because he assumed that I hadn't packed I will make him wait a second just to prove him wrong. I'll make this a teachable moment as my mother likes to call them teaching him not to make assumptions about me. I notice him open his laptop as I walk back into the living room with my suitcase. He knows how to have a good time, but he has that laptop with him everywhere. That is one of the things that my mom loves about him. He is a good example of balance, so she says. He was consumed in his work that he didn't even notice that I was ready, so I blurted it out, "I'm ready." "Wow, so you were ready after all. I guess an apology is in order." "Yes, and I am waiting," I say as I stand near the door with my arms folded as he pushes pass me opening the door. "Well, keep waiting now let's go."

When we arrived at the airport my mom and Samuel were already there waving us to join them. For once she was too indulged in her conversation with Samuel that she didn't mention my tardiness that was not my fault for once, but she would never believe it. We sat for about five minutes when it was time to board. Before I could get comfortable on the plane, we had landed. We got to the hotel checked in and planned to meet in the lobby within an hour. Bryson kept his word by truly giving direction as we got to the room keeping on schedule to be ready within an hour. I didn't mind it, but I really didn't like people telling me what to do. So, I needed to teach him another lesson. When I walked out of the bathroom wearing my pink panty set, I had to quickly remind him that we had a schedule to stick to. He didn't like that at all, but I found it quite hilarious because I was doing exactly what he directed me to do, which is keep to the schedule. To make matters worse, when we arrived at the lobby on time my mom and Samuel were twenty minutes late. Not trying to find out what caused them to be late I just indulged in a little fun at the slot machines. After I lost twenty dollars, I was ready for dinner, we all headed to the restaurant.

Upon our arrival to dinner everyone seemed to be enjoying themselves. After dinner I found this boat ride for us to do so we headed over there.

Bryson and I lead the way holding hands enjoying the scenery. He and I made plans to get up early to have some time alone which I was excited for. When we got to the boat ride my mom thought it would be a good idea if we both took our own separate boats, and we did. On the ride the conversation got a little more serious than usual. "So, Vanessa, you've told me that you like the idea of a big family, but could you explain to me how that looks to you?" "Married, five kids, a nice home, two dogs and lots of family trips." "Well, that is precise" (both laughing) I continued on to say, "Yeah, I don't have much family, so I've always wanted to have a big one if I ever did. What about you?" "Oh, beautiful, strong intelligent wife, to mother our three kids, a beautiful home and making many memories together but I can do without the dogs." I quickly reply, "No dogs, but you had one growing up?" "That is why I can do without, that dog use to shit all over the place not to mention he once did in my Jordan 1's that is when I knew I didn't want another one." He had the most gorgeous smile that sometimes had me mesmerized. "Well, that means we have to train our dogs not to shit all over our house" "So, I'm your husband in that in that scenario" "Definitely." "I love a woman who knows what she wants, that's a sexy trait." He said as he sat up in the boat howling like a wolf, having the guide turn around with this scared confused look on her face. I am not sure why I know she has seen crazier shit than that, we are in Vegas. I just saw a woman in the middle of a crowd wearing dental floss as clothing. We continued the boat ride as the tour guide tried to tell us about the scenery, but we continued to engage in our own conversation trying not to be obviously rude. At the completion of our ride, we found my mom and Samuel to walk the strip. We stopped sightseeing as if we all hadn't been here several times in the past; however, we had not experienced it with each other so it may it a fresh new experience.

Later that night as we were passing this chapel, my mom stopped asking to go in, confused as to why of all places she would want to stop there. Trying to keep everyone moving ahead, Samuel walks in grabbing my mom's hand. Now irritated, I follow behind trying to figure out what the hell they are trying to do. When this weird guy walks in wearing thong sandals and a beach hat requesting to help, I immediately tell him that we were just leaving. However, my mom and Samuel began to ask prices. Trying to convince my mom that she has lost her mind making an irrational decision in the heat of the moment was not the best look for her. She still was adamant about moving forward with marrying this man. I mean she just met him, I tried to beg her to give it some more time, but she wasn't hearing me. "Bryson, you're just going to stand there allowing her to make such an impulsive decision." "Woman, Ms. Gyles is Ma, how am I supposed to tell her what to do? Besides, she has made some pretty good decisions in her lifetime." "Oh, just shut up." I freakishly wanted to end this trip but had no power to. After fifteen minutes of pleading my case, I decide to sit in the back, arms folded cringing, refusing to stand beside her as she does the dumbest thing in the world when out of now where I hear in unity "GOTCHA!!" Apparently, my mom wanted to get me back for pushing her in the pool with the dolphins. Well, it worked. With me still pouting while everyone else laughed all the way back to the hotel, I wanted to know where my mom found this new sense of humor.

When we arrived at the hotel, Bryson and I decided to stay at the casino for a while to have a few drinks. Before I knew it, it was five in the morning, and we hadn't been to the sleep. Even a night owl such as I was tired. I could tell Bryson was on his last boost of energy as we held each other up in efforts of making it to the room. As soon as our body touched the bed we were out. This time when the alarm went off at eight, we both decided to ignore it. When we finally woke up at twelve, we showered but this time allowing him to take a peak at the set I was going to wear today. We took our time this morning but neither of us minded it. When we were finally ready to leave the room, I called my mom who had been up and out since seven this morning. They were now ready for lunch; she let us know they have made reservations to meet them. We did just that, besides we were starving. After lunch we had no true, itinerary just going with the flow of the day. My mom and Samuel decided to venture off to do their own thing, we did as well.

Later that night we had plans to go to this beautiful restaurant that overlooked this water fountain that does a water show at night. Bryson got dressed before me because he wanted to get to the restaurant on time to ensure that we didn't lose our reservations. I was honestly drained from the heat not to mention the endless walking that I wouldn't have mind to sit in the room and order room service but somehow, I gathered enough energy to get dressed. My mom sent a picture of what she was wearing so I had to be sure to really put some effort into my look tonight. Besides Bryson was looking like a chocolate candy bar when he left; therefore, I really wanted to look nice. Once I was dressed in my long multi-color body con, spaghetti strap dress, and heels I went towards the lobby to meet my mom and Samuel. When I get to the lobby, I am greeted by just my mom as Samuel went ahead with Bryson. On our way to the restaurant my mom was telling me how happy she was with Samuel and glad that Bryson and I are getting a head start on things. It felt good to see her happy, but I was nervous ever since last night that she would rush into something with this man. Although, I was happy for her I didn't want her to rush.

Dinner was beautiful, the food was delicious, and the service was amazing. Afterwards we decided to watch the water show. As we were getting closer to our stopping point Bryson grabbed my hand. "Vanessa, this weekend is everything that I could have asked for. I enjoy spending time with you, creating memories and just overall being happy. You are truly one of a kind, you embody strength, courage, love, passion, and beauty. I love you for being you and accepting me for being me. Your friendship is the foundation that sparked a love that I cannot live without. I guess, what I am trying to say is…." When I watched Bryson kneel on one knee requesting me of all people to be his wife, I felt the room around me disappear while I was captivated by just him in that moment. I soaked it all in trying to remember exactly how he looked, the exacted words he said, the gorgeous smile he had plastered on his face. "Fuck yeah, I'll be your wife" I was ecstatic beyond belief. It felt surreal that just a month ago, I felt like someone who had no family at all now joining a family that I have always loved preparing to create one of my own. In the mist of the highlight of my night, my mother who had been in on this entire surprise came over to hug while congratulating me.

We stood out there for a while allowing me to gather my emotions. When we got into the car to head towards the hotel I asked if I could share with my girls. Of course, I gave them a facetime call and before I could utter a word all I could hear was "Yasss, welcome to the fucking family!" "Congratulations, Vanessa." Apparently, he told them about it when they were in town a few weeks back. I am surprised that they were able to keep it a secret being that since they have left our conversations picked up heavy. I mean no one slipped up anything especially Shynelle. When we pulled up to the hotel ending the call with the ladies, I was in a bliss that I could not describe. That night, I didn't want to do anything but spend time with the man who loved me enough to request my hand in marriage to start a family of our own. I was happy because although that is something that I have always desired. I just never in a million years envisioned it for my life. I guess you don't have to have it all together to have the life you want.

Over the next few days, I was still in utter disbelief of how my life was changing. I was doing things that I never imagined would happen for me with the support of my girls which makes it all worth it. As I was preparing for work this morning, I received a call from my mom who was panicking about meeting Samuel's daughter tonight. I tried to convince her that everything would be fine, but she wanted to make a great impression. In my entire life, I have never seen my mother take a tiny bit of interest in a man. She has always been so work driven focusing on making sure that I had everything I needed plus more that she never gave anyone the time of day. I used to feel bad for the men who tried to approach her because she was cold when letting them down. It's the attorney in her that is just straight to the point. When I got older, I asked her why she never dated but she didn't say much. I later learned that when she got pregnant at a young age with me, her family disowned her forcing her to struggle to raise me on her own and although I have no recollection of that hardship, I believe it still lives presently in her mind today. This is why she has tried extremly hard to teach me that I can do thing on my own, striving to ensure that I was independent.   Although she succeeded in making me independent, I still have always longed for that family relationship. I have never had that conversation with her because I never wanted to make her feel bad because it is not her fault that her family did not want to be a part of our lives. I remember years ago walking in the room on her as she received a letter from her mom. I am not sure what it said but I remember seeing the pain behind her tears when I opened the door. I was about six at the time, so I didn't know what to do but run to hug my mother. So, to see her finally letting go to live in the moment aiming to be happy makes my heart smile. She deserves to experience every bit of happiness that she is feeling right now. After I calmed her down, I ensured her that I would be there promptly to accompany her which seemed to work.

After work, as promised, I went straight to my mother's house. When I arrived, she was already at the door waiting on me. "You look gorgeous mom. "Thanks baby, thanks for coming I truly appreciate it." "Of course, anything for my favorite girl." We hug, then I run upstairs to change so that I could help her finish setting up. We were having a small little dinner just Samuel, his daughter, my mom, and me. When the doorbell rang, my mom got a little nervous, so I went to the door. After greeting Samuel and Lyla, his daughter I walk back to the dining room with a smirk on my face causing my mom to be a slight bit confused. When they entered the room, my mom had the biggest smile on her face walking over to hug Lyla who was the young lady from the airport serving the mimosa's back during our Christmas trip. "Wow, dad you really hit the jackpot with this one." Samuel confused at everything that was going on around him, we decided to catch him up letting him know how we had already previously met. Such a small world but it truly made dinner a breeze. The connection across the table was there, no forcing just there.

Later that night as I was heading home, I stopped to get gas so that I wouldn't have the hassle of rushing in the morning. When I arrived home, I straighten up a bit and prepared my things for the next morning. I am not sure what made me do it but the next morning I wasn't rushing out of the house, I had time to sit to enjoy a cup of coffee. At work, was a typical day with seven cleanings. It wasn't too bad, but I was ready to go by the end of my shift. After work I had the urge to do a little self-care, so I went to get a pedicure. By the time I was finished I stopped at this little food spot nearby to grab a bite to eat. When I got there, it was chill, deciding to sit to eat. While waiting for my food I responded to Yazmine's text regarding the new grand re-opening of the restaurant. By the time I responded my food had arrived; I sat there eating while watching some show they had playing on the television. Not sure what it was called but I couldn't take my eyes off it. I sat there enjoying my meal while watching the show when I received a call from Bryson who was out of town for work again. He and I talked until I arrived home for the night.

Chapter 13: Creepy Sh**

Since I have been back from visiting Ms. Gyles, work life has been on overload. I have been extremely busy trying get things done working late every day; I am drained. On top of that Lisa called me last night in a fright because her husband had been in an accident. I was with her all night until she found out her husband would be fine. He will be able to go home this afternoon. I wanted to take the day off but with Lisa out on top of all the deadlines we have this week, I could not afford to be off. I had plans to take Mrs. Thomas shopping this afternoon but I really think that I am going to have to reschedule. When I get to work, I find the assignment that Lisa was working on that so that I could complete it because it is due at noon. Luckily, she does her work as well as she talks crap because I really didn't have to do much. She is the best assistant director. I finish up the work that I must complete plus take two extra conference calls and a staff meeting. By the end of the day, I was drained not to mention sleepy, but I forgot to call Mrs. Thomas to cancel so I decided to just go ahead to take her. After we finished shopping, and helping her put the groceries away, I somehow dozed off on her couch. I am not sure how long I was sleeping but I woke up with a cover and the smell of something amazing cooking. "Hi sleepy head, you dozed off right after you took a call. You were looking so peaceful that I didn't want to disturb you. I have made some soup if you are hungry." "Thank you, Mrs. Thomas, but I really should be getting home I have to get up early in the morning." "I already know that's why I have packed you a bowl to go; there should be enough in there for you to take to lunch as well. That can be one less thing that you have to worry about little bit." "Thank you, Mrs. Thomas," I give her the biggest hug, grabbing the bag that she has prepared for me.

When I got home, I crack open my laptop to work, for a couple of hours. I received a text from Nathan. I never respond to this man, which is I am not sure why he hasn't gotten the hint that I am not interested. I hate that I gave him my number as I have already told him that I am not interested. I'll be 31 this year; if love happens, I will be okay but if it, doesn't I will also be just fine. But what I do know is it will not be with him. I was about to lay down for the night when I get a call. I tried to ignore it, but it rang again so I thought maybe it was Lisa and I had to make sure everything was okay. I get my phone and it was Mr. Thomas letting me know that Mrs. Thomas was being rushed to the hospital. He let me know not to worry but I know that his nephew who usually helps them out works a lot out of town and I believe she mentioned earlier that he was now which is why he wasn't able to take her to the store this afternoon. I let him know that I would meet him at the hospital. Even though he requested that I not come he just wanted to inform me I still got dressed and headed to the hospital. Before I could get out of my complex, I got a call back from Mr. Thomas letting me know that everything is alright and that she would be back home tomorrow so not to come. I let him know I would be by tomorrow to check on them. By this time its 11p.m. and I am exhausted I believe I was sleep before my head hit my pillow.

The next morning my alarm went off at 4:12 a.m. to get ready for the gym, but my body wouldn't let me get up no matter how hard I tried. I decided not to work out this morning to get another hour of sleep. By the time it was time for me to get up for work I was still tired, but I had just enough energy to get ready for the day. I made the decision that this weekend I would take the time to rest, no work, no running around just time to get refocused on me. It was a pleasant surprise; work was a breeze this Friday I even got off a little early which doesn't happen too often. As promised, I planned stop by to check on Mrs. Thomas but I stopped at this flower shop up the street from their home to get her some roses because they are her favorite. "Those are some beautiful flowers held by a beautiful woman. Hi, I'm Ken." I turn around noticing this beautiful specimen of a man smiling at me with his khaki slacks and polo shirt. He was well groomed, flawless brown skin, low fade and his goatee looks as though he uses Shea Moisture products because it has the perfect shine. "Hi there, thank you but they're not for me." I must have been in a daze because he didn't ask me that. "Well, we are going to have to change that." He walks over picks up some roses along with the flowers that he already had in is hand and purchases them. After he pays, he hands me the roses that he just picked up gifting them to me. "Thank you, Ken that is really sweet of you." "You never told me your name." "I'm sorry this week has been crazy; I'm Shynelle." "I get it. It's nice to meet you Mrs. Shynelle." "Oh no, its Ms." Okay he thinks he is slick, but it made me look at his ring finger and there was no ring. "I have somewhere I have to be, but do you think we could exchange numbers?" I was hesitant but I decided what the hell and gave it to him. As he was walking off, I received a call, and it was him making sure I gave him the right number.

As I was pulling up in front of Mr. and Mrs. Thomas house, I notice the car that Ken got into pull up behind me, so I was on guard at this point. I called Mr. Thomas to let him know what was going on keeping my car running but I had nowhere to go because he has blocked me in the driveway. This is some creepy shit which is why I find it hard to date these days. Why in the hell did this man just follow me here? Mr. Thomas opens the door giving me a slight relief but there isn't much that he could do. Mr. Thomas walks out the house knocks on my window as he walks pass approaching Ken's car even if that is his name. When Ken gets out, he has that same goofy smile on his face but the last thing I expected for them to do was hug. I felt a little more comfortable deciding to open my car door but before I could get out, I hear Mr. Thomas "Hey little bit, come here and meet my nephew." "Oh, good I thought you were a creep stalking me" I put a smile on my face, but my heart was still racing, and hands were shaking. "Oh, I do apologize I honestly was wondering why you were here too you know men get stalked also." "So, you two have met?" "Yes, unc she is the pretty lady I just told you I met at the store which is why I am just a little late getting here." Mr. Thomas patted me on the shoulder with the biggest smile on his face and I couldn't help but to smile back because that was very flattering. "So how do you know my aunt and uncle?" "I met them at my job when I moved here, and they haven't been able to get rid of me." "Oh, so you are the young lady that has been helping them since I have been out of town wow that's crazy. But thank you so much; It takes a special woman to help people that they haven't known long the way you have been helping my family. It's safe to say that I am no longer just captured by your beauty."

I stayed over Mr. and Mrs. Thomas house longer than I initially planned. I did say that I was going to take this weekend to do what I wanted and sitting there enjoying conversation with Ken was exactly what I needed and wanted. We ended the night at a restaurant for dinner. We also made plans for tomorrow afternoon since he has already made plans to help his uncle fix some things around their house in the moring. A man who is not only brilliant but takes the time to help his family is so attractive to me. I didn't know they even existed.

The next morning, I slept in until about ten, but I still sat in the bed binge watching tv, which I never get to do, but one of my favorite hobbies. I really need to stop watching all these crime shows. I think that is why I am always so jumpy. But it is the one thing that makes me feel close to my mother. My dad would tell me all the time how my mother use to enjoy watching those shows with me as a little girl. He never speaks badly about her even though she left him when I was three. I do not have any memories of her but pictures. After my dad waited for her for about a year, he got a job offer in California which he took resulting in us moving from South Carolina when I was five. A few months later he met his current wife who did not have any children of her own at the time but treated me as her child. I love her for that because I had never needed for a mother figure. When I was thirteen, she and my father were blessed with my little brother and a year later my sister. I was so happy to finally have siblings even though I already felt like it because I grew up with Yazmine and Bryson. Our fathers are best friends, and our mothers obviously built a strong relationship.

After relaxing for hours, I get out the bed to eat. After finishing my bagel, I began cleaning listening to music. By noon I was in a spotless house to continue my relaxation, I ran a bubble bath and gave myself a facial. By the time I finished I finally got dressed to head to the nail shop. I luckily had an appointment therefore I didn't have a wait at all. When I finished, I did a little retail therapy because the nail shop is in a shopping center. After a fun filled, relaxing day I head home to get dressed for my date tonight with Ken who called to make sure we were still on for today.

Later that evening, Ken came to pick me up from my house. Normally I would never allow a new person into my safe space, but I trust him because I know his aunt and uncle who spoke highly of him even before I coincidently met him yesterday. He showed up to my home wearing a burgundy fitted suit, smelling amazing and wearing that gorgeous smile which isn't goofy at all. I was wearing a brown body fitting dress, heels, and a burgundy purse. I noticed it but he made a comment about our coordinating. I didn't know where were going; he just told me to dress up, so I did. When we pull up to this restaurant it was a beautiful place that I had never been before. When we walked in, he spoke with the host. As we were directed to seating, we passed all the tables and were directed to this private room in the back that was drop dead gorgeous. I don't know how this man was able to put this together in such a short period of time, but I was amazed. I had to take several mental pictures because I needed proof for myself that something like this was done for me because I wasn't sure if I were dreaming. I was so appreciative that I turned hugging him like he had given me the best gift in the world. "Well, I wonder how you are going to act the rest of the night." "This is really sweet Ken; I have never had anything like this happen for me. I mean I see it for other people all the time but never in a million years has anyone done anything like this for me. Thank you for putting so much thought into tonight". "You are welcome, just wait until our second date." "The night is just beginning; how do you know after tonight you will want to have a second date with me." "I knew after last night that there is not another date that I don't want to go on without you". I began blushing and I pretty sure he can tell because like my father I fare skin and turn red quickly. He didn't say anything he just smiled pulling out my chair. As we talked for hours at dinner; I learned that he was raised by his uncle and aunt who took him in after his grandmother passed. His parents gave him away as a baby because they didn't have time for him. So, he has been with his aunt and uncle since he was seven. He has a very successful business selling commercial real-estate properties that he does across the country which is why he travels as much as he does. He told me how happy he was that my uncle and aunt met me. "My aunt and uncle talk about you all the time but they never called you by your name, so I would have never known who you were." "Yeah, for some reason they call me little bit, but I am taller than both of them." "You know how older folks are, they can't remember names, so they make them up." I sit at dinner enjoying it with a man who has not only good looks but great conversation. He is absolutely a great catch. After an evening filled with great conversation, delicious food, surprises, and good company we decided to call it a night because he has a flight in a few hours.

When I made it home, I was on a natural high that I just sat on the couch thinking if I really experienced such joyous night or, I am dreaming. Later that night as I was watching yet another crime shows, my phone vibrated scaring the shit out of me. It was Ken calling letting me know that he was at the airport but how he enjoyed spending time with me on today and apologies that he had to leave tonight, promising to make some changes in his schedule to have more time with me. We talked until his plane was about to board. Right before he was about to let me go, he asked, "So, I don't really date. I mean I haven't in such a while because I have been trying to get my business to the point it is now, and I may have a bit of trust issues. There is something about you that draws me to you, and I would love to keep that in my life. My uncle has taught me to speak my mind and let it be known what I want and work for it.

Well, I know I want you. So, I am saying all this to ask is it safe to say that we are dating? I want to make you my woman and if it is too soon, I just want to know if it's okay to say that we can work on making that happen?" "Yes, I like that. I think it is okay to say we are dating. We can see where things go." I have no experience in dating, so I believe that means to continue to get to know one another. I am open to that. We ended the call after we talked a little longer. To describe this moment was nothing short of utopia in the way that I was felling right now. I have never been the woman that got the dude. I was always the one they approached with the stupid line "so what's up with your friend". But one day out of nowhere I got this urge to take care of me and ever since that day my life has been different. I love everything about the changes I have made. And it's not even just the weight lost because I was being approached before that. I gained a confidence that apparently attracted others to me. Surprisingly, I am interested to see if we could develop that relationship that he is speaking of. He is everything and more that the Thomas's described in him. They never tried to play match maker with the two of us never even trying to introduce us but when we did meet, and they saw our connection Mr. Thomas claimed that he already knew we would be a great match if we ever met. Mrs. Thomas never said much just smiled. They claim that if we were to meet that wanted it to happen organically. I am pleased that it did.

Chapter 14: Date Night

Last night, Terrance asked me out on a date. In such a short period our lives have changed drastically. We went from working constantly, to having Cameron residing with us full time and now just not having time for each other. Although things are different, we have noticed the need to make time for one another. Our communication has gotten back to where it needs to be not to mention the love is presently residing within our home. So, when he asked me out tonight; I took him up the offer. I have had so much help in Mason with this restaurant that I have not had any stressful moments in a while. I was feeling optimistic about the outcome of this place. I am enjoying this watching it turn into something beautiful right before my eyes. I just hope that when it opens it bring that same type of energy.

The contractors meeting was short and went well. The rest of the afternoon I cleared my schedule to do something that I have been dreading doing for a while. I first went to get a manicure and pedicure. Afterwards I went to a few stores to find something to wear tonight. I hadn't been out in so long that I couldn't remember the last time I went shopping for myself. I was in the stores for hours trying on clothes.

There was one lady who was talking to me letting me know how she lost over one hundred pounds, so she was in dire need of a new wardrobe. She started asking my opinion on things and before you knew it, we were shopping buddies. She let me know how she was new to the city as her and her family moved here for her husband's job so now, she is starting over. She was so relatable, and pleasant to talk with. When we decided on our outfits of purchase, I gave her my business card and invited her to the grand reopening of the restaurant.

When I left from shopping, I was just in time to make my hair appointment. When I arrived, I was met by my stylist who I had gone to in the past, but it has been a while to say the least. When I sat in her chair, she wasn't pleased with how damaged I had let my hair get but showed me several styles that she thought I would like. I decided on the short ear length bob. I was panicking; however, I trusted her to make it nice. I can't remember all that she was doing but by the end when she gave me the mirror, I was surprising shocked at how much I loved it. When I walked out of her salon, I had a new walk. That confidence that I had been missing was creeping back up my spine and I was walking tall again. I was feeling like a newer improved version of myself, yep, I was the shit, and no one could tell me otherwise. I hadn't told Terrance that I was cutting my hair because before I sat in the stylist chair, I wasn't sure if I was going to go through with it or not. So, when I got home, I showered preparing for the night. I bought this sexy red gown that strapped around the neck that had an opening showing just enough cleavage to be sexy for my man but appropriate for dinner. I pulled out my make-up, jamming some oldies while I finished getting dressed. I finished just in time for my Uber. Terrance had made it home to change prior to my getting home from my hair appointment so I let him know that I would meet him there. This was a work event, but his work events are for the most are partially fun. It wasn't the most ideal date, but it was something.

When I pull up to the venue, I call Terrance to let him know that I was there. When I walked in, I spotted him looking handsome as usual. When he got closer to me his mouth dropped. I couldn't tell it he liked it or not but then he started grinning showing every tooth he had in his mouth. "Hey, miss, my name is Terrance, may I dance with you tonight?" "Sorry, I am waiting on my husband." "That's cool, I'm married too. This could be our little secret." Role playing when you are married is always fun so that was our thing for tonight only getting out of character when his coworkers were around. By the end of the night, we had flirted with one another so much that we were both ready to leave the event to go home because the sexual tension had intensified throughout the night. We pulled up to the house and into the garage with not a second to waste ripping each other clothes off. Soon realizing that car sex was just not as comfortable as it used to be we decided to make our way into the house. Not getting as far as to the kitchen when we tried to give it a second attempt. Before I knew it, I was laid out on the island wearing nothing, but a thong covered in whip cream. Everything was going well when Mason, who said he wouldn't be back until tomorrow walked in leaving us in total embarrassment. He quickly left out, but my natural reaction was to cover up resulting in me kicking Terrance in the eye and me falling of the kitchen island inflicting pain on the both of us. Terrance holding his eye came over to see if I were okay and I was fine, but I knew that bruise would be on my leg in the morning. I kicked him hard, so I quickly grabbed some ice for him to place on it.

Later that night, I went to clean our mess up hoping not to run into Mason. It appears that he locked himself in his room trying to forget any image that he saw tonight. After I finish cleaning, I went back to our room to Terrance who was now asleep. He was laying on the eye that I kicked so I couldn't tell if it left a scar or not. My fall left a bruise not to mention it was sore. The next morning, I woke up before Terrance to shower. When I walked out the shower there he was standing with a black eye "now how the hell do I explain this at work today?" I made extreme efforts not to laugh but it was so hard not to. "It's not funny" "I am sorry baby, but it is hard not to laugh." I walk over giving him a hug inviting him in the shower with me finishing up from where we stopped last night minus the theatrics. By the time we sat at the breakfast table, Terrance was all smiles dressed for work eating breakfast as Mason walked in shaking his head. "Yall are getting too old to be doing whatever it is yall were trying last night, just look at your face bruh" Terrance and I locked eyes immediately bursting out in laughter. Sometimes all you can do is laugh then move on.

Later that day, Mason and I had a cooking class. He felt that I should have a little knowledge of what goes on the kitchen being that I own the restaurant. He was so excited for me to enter his world of cooking that there was no awkwardness surrounding last night incident. When we arrived at the class, we waited on two other individuals. The young lady teaching the class was in her early twenties playing some cool hip-hop music and she served wine which made it even better. We were preparing lamb chops with mustard-thyme sauce on a bed of mashed potatoes and asparagus. It sounded delicious so I am glad Mason was here to help because I had no idea as to what I was doing. The class was fun and the instructor was full of energy with a passion for her work. I thoroughly enjoyed every minute of it. At one point in the class this older lady went to the middle of the class with the instructor and began dancing. She was on her second bottle, so she was turned up to the maximum, but I was here for all of it, so I cheered her on.

As we were cleaning up, Mason came over to introduce the instructor letting me know that she would be a great sous chef for our restaurant. I wasn't opposed to the idea, so I planned for us to discuss the position plus salary. When we arrived home, Terrance was there watching the game in his chill attire still gorgeous as ever, even with the black eye. I brought him some of the food we made and of course he gave Mason all the credit, but I knew that it was the sprinkled love that I put into it making taste so delicious. I joined Terrance and Mason as they watched the game. Later that evening, we did a facetime call with Cameron who looks as though he has grown so much in such a short period. His dad had to step away for a call when all I heard was "Yaz guess what?" "What Cameron?" "I have a girlfriend and she got a big booty but don't worry she smart too." "Cameron who told you that you could have a girlfriend. And does your mother know?" "I haven't told her yet, but I think she knows since she saw us hanging out the other day when she picked me up from basketball practice." "Oh well, what do you all do that makes you two a couple?" "Yaz, just talk but I do want to take her on a date. So, I was thinking, could you talk to my parents for me." "How about this, I'll just sit here as your support so that you can tell them yourself. Go get your mom, I hear your dad coming now." "What is Cameron trying to do now Yazmine" Laughing because Cameron always tries to put me in the middle of something, but it never works; however, I always sit in to support him I don't know why but I give him the courage to talk with them. By the end of the call, Terrance was happy, but Cameron's mom was not so pleased. I get it, who wants their baby boy to be in lala land over a girl. However, they did come to the agreement that he could take her on a chaperoned date if her parents allow it with Terrance putting money in his account to fund the date.

The next day Cameron sent me a text letting me know that he would be going on his date this weekend; therefore, he would need something nice to wear. Funny thing is he sent a picture of the exact outfit and shoes that he believes he would look nice in attached to the body of his text. I gathered the hint, so I ordered the items to be sent to his home. I spoiled him but I couldn't help it, he was just as much my baby as he was his parents. Later that morning I met with the instructor from yesterday as scheduled, feeling very enthusiastic about the success of this restaurant. I finally received the paperwork for Mason so as he was in the kitchen talking with the contractor who was just about finished, I called him to meet with me once he had the opportunity. I sat the paperwork down for him to read, when he finished, he looked up at me in disbelief not knowing if it were real. Once I explained to him that I indeed was offering him a percentage of the restaurant he fell into my arms giving me the sincerest hug. I felt good to be in a position to be able to give to him what wasn't given to me.

Chapter 15: Enticing Conversation

Yazmine called yesterday inviting me to her grand opening but it's not for another month. I am pleased to find out that Mason is now the head chef. He truly deserves it. I hired him to cater a work event last summer and everyone boast and raved on the quality presentation and taste. He always had the skill of cooking but lacked presentation which was gained at culinary school. Leaving work this Friday evening I feel drained as usual, but I gain burst of energy as I was leaving the office because Ken has been talking about this special weekend, he has planned out for us the past two weeks now. He was raised by Mr. Thomas; he is a true gentleman and a man of his word; however, he really does have some trust issues that he needs to work through. When I arrive home, I pull out my luggage to put in the outfits that Vanessa, Yazmine and I picked out last night on our call. When Yazmine met Ken via facetime, she was thrilled that he lived up to the "hype" that she claims I gave him. As soon as I told her that he had a special weekend planned for us I received a package with a note on the box "get you some d". I was so embarrassed that that the delivery man had to see that when delivering it. When I opened the package finding the cutest lingerie set. When she asked was, I going to take it, I said no as my typical bashful self when it comes to stuff like that but in my mind, I had every intention of bringing it just in case which is why I packed it with the rest of my clothing. All I know is that we are going somewhere out of the state. I was told nothing too major because I cannot afford to take any more days off anytime soon which sucks because I have tons of paid time off built up its just the workload of being a director takes more time and dedication than other positions. I am, however, going to take a half of a day on Monday and work out of the office just so that we don't have to rush back. After I was getting out the shower, I received a call from Ken letting me know that he will be here in twenty minutes. I didn't have time to put on any makeup, therefore, I put a little something together. Yazmine being the toughest person that I know and having all brothers you would never think that she is the diva of the bunch. She loves to shop and have her make up done even if it's just a little bit which is why we all knew something was wrong with her. I have always told her she resembles a beautiful model and she is very tall. She taught us how to do our make up when we were in high school. Vanessa caught on quickly; me however, it took me a little more time but once I got the hang of it, I loved it. As I grabbed my last bag from the room Ken knocked at the door. "Hey love, are you ready?" "I am, just grabbed my last bag." "Ha, you really bring your own sheets when you travel huh." "I already told you; I hate hotels which is ironic because my father loved to travel when I was a child." "I get it, you are kind of OCD I've noticed but your cleanliness is a good trait" "funny guy, I see" "yeah but let's go before we miss our flight". When we got to the airport, he let me know that we were going to Miami which excited me even more just because I knew Yazmine would come to see me no matter where we are. Just as I was about to text "I'm so glad to have you to myself this weekend uninterrupted" I put my phone away smiling. I guess I will just have to let her know the situation; I just hopes she will understand.

When we arrived in Miami, we went straight to our room which was a high-rise condo in downtown Miami. It was beautiful. On our flight we discussed a summer trip with Dubai as an option. I didn't know he was as serious but as soon as we made it to the hotel, he booked the trip for us. I have never been there, hell in my adult life I really have not traveled much at all. I wasn't so sure that he and I would make it to the summer. He really got upset with an older gentleman around Mr. Thomas age for speaking to me. It made me a bit frustrated and scared that his trust issues were truly something a little bit more serious, but I didn't want to overanalyze things as I usually do so I decided to let it go. Overall, I like him as he is spontaneous, not wasting anytime when he makes his mind up on what he wants to do. I guess opposites do attract because his behavior so resembles the Vanessa when it comes to the love for traveling.

We have dinner reservations at this beachfront restaurant, so I go get dressed. When Ken walks out of the bathroom with his towel wrapped around his waist, I tried to pretend to put my earrings on when he caught my eyes staring. I wasn't even embarrassed, shockingly. I think that turned him on because he walked over standing behind me as I was now standing in front of the mirror making sure my makeup looked okay. He then grabbed me by the waist kissing me on my neck. Yeah, it's been a long time and he and I have been dating for a little while now I think this is going to be the weekend. As he walked away grabbing my ass that is looking nice in this dress if I must say so myself, I began to smile. I wait a little longer for him to get dressed. When he finished, he walked out looking like he just stepped off the front page of a magazine. That man is gorgeous, it was still hard to believe that he wants me.

Leaving the hotel, we run into this beautiful young lady "Hey Ken" "Oh, what's up Mona…" before he could finish, she runs up to hug him. Oh no, I knew it was too got to be true; I was getting pissed. My natural reaction kicked in, so I snatched my hand away from him, now holding my purse with both hands in front of me. But to my surprise he pulls her off him, grabs my hand and introduces me to her. "Mona, this is my future wife Shynelle" "Hi, nice to meet you…" She rolled her eyes folding her arms refusing to shake my hand. "Oh, so just some months ago you weren't ready to be in a relationship but now you have a future wife. I find that odd." "No, just a few months ago I told you I didn't want a relationship with you which I told you upfront. But look, I have this beautiful woman waiting for dinner so we must go so I can feed her. You enjoy your night and be safe." He grabbed my hand leading me out the door. The look on her face displayed astonishment by his response. This behavior intrigued me a bit. I just witnessed him claiming me as his woman not allowing another woman to question it was such a turn on, I just wanted to go back to the room to let him know.

When we got in the car, I heard him say, "I apologize to you for that. I hope that doesn't change your stance with us." "No, we all have a past but you are informing her of her position in your life as of today makes me confident that there might be a future for us. I have never met a man who has shown me that he likes me the way you do. But you didn't have to call me your future wife we have only been dating for a little while." "That's all the time I need to know that you will be my wife, sooner than later. I just know you like to analyze things and overthink, so I am giving you the time you need to get to know all you need to know about me." "I know all I need to know Ken" He smiled, kind of blushing when I said that. "Well, that's good to know." When we made it to the restaurant there was a table set up for us near the beach which was so beautiful. He really pays attention to detail, having the flowers that I told him that I like the first day that we met. We sat at dinner talking for over two hours. When we finished, we decided to take our conversation to the beach. I was able to tell him how I felt about not having my biological mother be a part of my life. "I sit up late at night watching crime tv shows because my father told me my mom use to watch them all the time. I don't really didn't think I had an interest in them at first, yet I have grown to like them; however, they are why I am always so jumpy. But truthfully it is the only thing that I have of her so no matter how I try to stop something in me will not allow me to." I felt a tear, but he grabbed me close before it could even fall down my cheek. He made me feel special. "Sometimes the ones we love don't know how to love us back, but family can form with whomever you choose. You were fortunate enough to have a bonus mother. But I understand, there is nothing like wanting the love of a parent. I didn't have either of my parents. That shit hurt me for years until I was able to sit down with them after years of Uncle Thomas trying to get me to speak with them. Once I did, I received so much closure. My parents just were not equipped for parenting which is why I am thankful that they gave me to my grandmother. And then that my uncle and his wife were able to carry on that parental role when she was gone. I love them for that. I am no longer carrying around that pain. I speak to them, but I keep my distance because all they want from me now is money. My parents are my uncle and aunt who will never have to worry about a thing. May I ask you something?" "Yes." "Do you know why your mother left and have you tried to reach out to her?" "Well, for years my dad told me that she had a lot going on but when I was in high school, he finally told me the truth. He cheated on her repeatedly, after she had me. When she found out that he was having an affair, I guess she just couldn't take it anymore. He believes the hurt on top of the postpartum was her final breaking point, so she left. He told me that he has her information if I ever wanted to meet her as she has tried since I've gotten older, but I felt as though she took her anger for my father out on me. I don't know if meeting her would be beneficial or detrimental to the woman that I am today. You know what I mean?" "Yeah but coming from someone who has experienced a similar situation. Not addressing that trauma does nothing but if you choose to it may alleviate some of the hurt that has been holding you back. I think you should consider meeting with her if that is still an option. No pressure, but honestly, I want us to go into our marriage not carrying hurt from the past." "How would that impact what we have?" "Oh trust, you may not recognize it, but your abandonment issues may very well impact your behavior, you just don't recognize it. I still have some ways to go myself." Sitting there pondering on what he just said really made me think. I really have dealt with that my entire life which is still living presently in my thoughts daily. "How do you know so much about this if you don't mind me asking?" "My uncle put me in counseling when I was younger. However, I stopped going after a few sessions. When I became a teenager, he felt the need for me to go back being that I was older. I wasn't into it at first but man after a while of participating, I learned a lot about myself. Counseling really helped change my mindset. I used to be just the type of guy that had no ambition, no drive, just lost. After letting go of some of that hurt, I realized I am enough to be the man I desired to be not the little boy my parents weren't able to love. By the time I finished high school I graduated top of my class with six scholarship, and eight school acceptance offers. Honestly, my aunt and uncle are my walking angels. I stopped going for years until my cousin died. I knew I needed help with coping with that, so I went for a period then too but with my schedule its hard to make time for it. I don't see anything wrong with helping myself get through this thing we call life. It's not always glamourous like its portrayed on tv you know." I sat there in total admiration indulged by this cultivated, intelligent, confident, intriguing, beautiful specimen of a man who captured not only my heart but also my mind.

The next morning, we woke up early because we decided to run on the beach. He woke up prior to me because he too is a morning person. I just don't understand how that is normal. I have to give myself a pep talk every day. We went for our run deciding to eat at one of the restaurants for breakfast. After breakfast we decided to go shopping and sightseeing all before noon. When we made it back to the room, we took a shower preparing for this all-white yacht event he booked for us. Looking for my swimsuit, the lingerie Yazmine bought me fell out. I picked it up quickly so that he wouldn't see it, but I believe he did. Last night, he assured me that he was in no rush to have sex so we could continue to take our time. That gave a sense of peace. I believe I was on a conversational high from listening to him talk stimulating my mind that I didn't want to mess it up with jumping into bed with him. After we were dressed, we leave to go to the yacht party. When we arrived, it was so beautiful yet again another thing that I have never done. I was enjoying the new adventures that he was introducing me to, glad that I have been opened to living for once in my life. When we made it to the top of the boat, I was bumped hard. I just knew it was that Mona girl starting some mess, so I turned around ready for it. "Gurrlll, you look so damn good!" It was Yazmine and Terrance. Terrance went over greeting Ken while I was sitting there in complete shock. He just continues to find ways to make me happy. After hugging my friend who I thought I wouldn't see, I walk over to Ken giving him the biggest hug. "Thank you". He hugged me back as we walked to find our table. "Why didn't you tell me about this Yazmine" "Bitch you know my ass cannot keep a secret from you. Terrance told me that we were going to an event for his job, so I had no clue until we got on the boat. Bitch I am so glad he was lying because his work events are sometimes boring. Apparently, he and Ken put this together." We were in mid-sentence when the DJ played one of our songs causing both of us to jump up showing out as only we know how to do when we link up. The guys really enjoyed our performance.

As the night was coming to an end, I hugged my best friend tightly who had to go due to a meeting she has scheduled early in the morning. I really enjoyed my night. When we got to the room Ken received a business call, so I took the opportunity to do some work as well. I worked for about an hour before receiving a call from Yazmine letting me know she made it home saying how much fun she had. She was right; we really enjoyed ourselves. When Ken was finished, I was drained wanting to stay in, but I gathered just enough energy to get dressed. When we didn't make it in time for our dinner reservations, we decided to bar hop which didn't last long because he again was a little too aggressive for my liking. There was a gentleman with his wife who walked in the bar before us, and he continued to open the door for us. This guy honestly believed that he was checking me out versus being a polite person. I was over it, so we jointly decided to go back to the room where he apologized for his behavior. I accepted hoping that tomorrow goes better than the night ended.

Chapter 16: Missing Piece

I still can't believe my surprise day with Shynelle, that I am elated about my walk through this morning. To get ready this morning, I played the song that got us out on the dance floor acting a fool. No matter how old a person gets, there is always that one song that gets them youthful. When I walked out the room, Mason was dressed and ready for the day. On our ride there, we both had excitement about the day. When we got to the restaurant, it was a sight to see. I felt like I was walking into a new place. It gave me this sense of pride. The place prior to had the décor of the previous owner but this time I felt that I would do it right. There were a few minor things that we found to be fixed but overall, we were prepared for the grand re-opening. Now, we just needed to get to the planning. Mason' s menu was prepared; now we just needed to pick a date. Once we finished up with the contractor, we sat down to pick a date. When we completed that, I began calling previous staff to see who would like to return which was an event within itself. I had one guy say yes to returning but had the craziest work schedule request. I could tell that he wouldn't be reliable, so I decided against his return. Then there was this lady who had me on hold for ten minutes just to get back on the phone not to negotiate a pay increase or benefits but only would take the job if she were only put on the schedule with the guy who was previously the bar tender. I was in disbelief of how she could request something so outlandish. When I told her that I wouldn't be able to make that promise she declined the position.

I stayed at the office a little longer than I planned but not too much longer. I felt accomplished I had gotten so much done. I was confident in the staff that I had returning and letting go of the ones that really should have been gone a long time ago. I posted the open positions which weren't many. I called Nyla to come in tomorrow, the young lady I helped seek employment. I believe she would be a great assistant manager. Eagerly, she accepted the interview. Now that that was done, I went home to prepare for dinner. I decided to take Terrance to one of those hip-hop cooking courses. When I arrived home, Terrance had a bouquet of flowers with a note that said (if for the booty I must get a black eye, I don't want it-Love your husband). I couldn't help but laugh because only he could say the dumbest things attached to the sweetest gestures. I change, do my make-up, and prepare to walk out the house when I receive a call from Terrance to wait so that we could ride together. He pulled up to the house about five minutes later. He runs to change in less than ten minutes and out the door we went. When we arrived at the class, we had a different instructor, well this time two, a male and female, who exuded energy and dance moves. We met a couple from Chicago who were in town visiting. We had so much fun with them we invited them to join us for drinks since they were looking for things to do in the city. The night was filled with laughter, drinks and fun with my husband who doesn't mind embarrassing himself on the dance floor. The guy is the life of the party with his forever hype girl. At one point in the night, everyone formed a circle around us cheering him on making him believe that he had the moves.

Luckily, the next morning I felt great. Terrance on the other hand woke up with a slight hang over. Good thing it was Saturday, so he didn't have work. When I arrived at the office, I waited for Nyla who was prompt and dressed as the CEO of the company. She exceeded my expectations in her interview, so I gave her the job. She agreed to start next week so that she could assist with the grand opening. In talking with her, she let me know that she had graduated so this position came at the perfect timing. I was happy for her that I decided to take her out for lunch. I was so impressed with this young lady, she really seemed to have it all together. I loved her tenacity and ambition to fight against the odds.

When lunch was over, I called to check on Terrance who was up heading to play basketball with some of his friends. I guess he wasn't that sick after all. With him being out, I went shopping for an outfit to wear to the grand opening. I tried on a few dresses at one store but none of them spoke to me, so I went to some more stores. Ending the shopping day with a new purse, shoes for Cameron, pants for Terrance, and no dress. I will try again another day, but I began to get hungry. I stopped to grab some food then headed home. When I got there, it was empty. Terrance was still hanging with the fellas and Mason was also hanging out. The joy of an empty house gave me the bright idea to blast the music, put on my comfortable pjs, grab a bottle of wine, and eat my dinner on the deck. My neighbor, the older gentleman, came out in his robe pretending to water his plants, but I knew he was just coming to be nosey. He waves with a mean look on his face as he walks back into the house. When I finished, I sat there for just a little longer admiring the view. Finally, I got up watched a little television. Crossing one of those crime episodes that Shynelle likes to watch I decided to give it a try which didn't last not even a minute before I changed it. I sat there searching for something to watch for ten minutes when I decided to cut the television off. I was sitting there discovering that I am not used to having time to myself leaving me not knowing what to do. So, I picked up my laptop, not knowing what to do I started checking my email which led to work so I decided to put the laptop away.

As I was closing my laptop my phone rings. "Yazmine, what are you doing?" "Oh nothing, just enjoying some me time." "You? I don't believe it." "Well, I am. What about you? How is my friend Ken?" "I just left the gym, and he is doing great. I called to tell you that I spoke with my biological mother the other day and it was just that." "What do you mean, how did it make you feel?" "Well, at first anxious when I was on the phone with her. But after a short period, I realized that she was just the woman who birthed me. We had no connection, and she really didn't seem to want a relationship with me she just needed to apologize to get it off her conscious. She is happily married having raised another man child." "Shynelle, I am glad you were able to speak with her because I know that you have needed that for as long as I have known you." "Oh, so when we were five you knew that?" "Bitch, you know what I mean." We both laughed continue talking about her experience of talking to her mom and how her stepmother stood by her side for the entire experience. It was great to see that my friend is continuing to find peace as well as happiness within her life. I love to watch her win in all aspects of life. By the time we completed our call, Terrance had made it home, showered and was now on the couch sitting next to me watching the game. So, I scooted over under him with my cozy blanket to watch the game with him. I couldn't quite fall asleep because of his jumping with many emotions at every play I decided to go to the room to take a bubble bath since Shynelle claims that they are so relaxing. I ran my bubble bath, grabbed my glass of wine and a book that I have been wanting to read for a while. Surprisingly it was soothing, creating the perfect amount of relaxation that I needed. I thoroughly enjoyed it. As the night was coming to an end, I ended my night on my laptop working, managing to put it away in a decent time for bed. By the next morning I was refreshed and ready to tackle the day. Today was filled with completing task for the house such as grocery shopping, cleaning, and laundry. I got up early when Terrance was heading out for the gym to begin cleaning. By the time he returned, I was folding the first load of laundry. After he showered, he took on the grocery shopping so he wouldn't be asked to fold clothes but that just meant one less thing for me. By the end of the night, I had a sparkling clean home and a refrigerator full of food, yet we still decided to go out for dinner. Once we finished dinner, we decided to take a long walk on the beach just admiring the beautiful sunset. Before long an hour had passed deciding to head home for the night. On our way home we stopped for a little dessert at this ice cream place that we have been discussing trying just never made the time. Well, it was okay, but I don't think I have to have it again. Terrance believes they purchased store bought ice cream and added toppings to make it look fancy. I would have to agree. By the end of the night, we ended on the couch watching some show on Netflix. We have never been the two that had much interest in watching television but for some reason that show had us engaged not wanting to turn it off. By the time we went to bed having made it through six episodes making plans to finish watching it together this week. When we were preparing for bed Terrance gave Cameron a call just as he does every night then we called it a night.

After a relaxing weekend, I was ready for the planning of the grand reopening. Nyla, as usual was prompt with ideas. It was nice to be excited about going to this restaurant again, and although my parents did not want to run this place it is great that someone in my family has a big interest in it. It makes all the stress worth it. I am eager to see opening night because Mason is going to show out. We have a photo shoot tomorrow for our website, and the restaurant. He and I make a great team which doesn't surprise me at all. Once we made the final decisions on the vision for opening night, finalized the invites and the menu, we move forward to notifying guest. The night before the grand opening we will have a soft opening for a few family and friends to give everyone a sneak peek of the restaurant. Also, for Mason to demonstrate his skill without the pressure of a large crowed. The next night will be the big event that we have been working so hard for. I was excited to see how everything turns out.

When we were leaving the restaurant for the night Mason informed me that he had found a place so he would be moving out soon. Terrance and I were in no rush for him to leave but I was still happy that he would still be close by. I was glad that he decided to stay making this place feel more like home. With everything in place, all I needed to do was find something to wear as well as get prepared for this photo shoot on tomorrow so when I left the restaurant, I went out on yet another shopping adventure which resulted in a successful trip finally. But just in true Yazmine fashion there just had to be a hiccup in my situation so I had to return to the restaurant. I was notified there was an issue with a part needed for the kitchen which is why we are now frantically trying to get it so that we can open. The inspector has given us a week before he will return giving us enough time so that we can keep the grand opening date; however, if we fail to get it in time this will result in us pushing it back until I don't know when being that the inspector next date will be at least a month out if we don't pass on his next visit. I was beginning to feel the stress again but before I would let it get the best of me, I took a moment to gather myself. I began calling around trying to help the workers locate the part that they are needing to finish the work, but I had no luck. Fortunately, just as I was hanging up with the million-part store Nyla barges in screaming "we found one!" "You found the part that they need?" "Yes, the company has shipped it overnight and will be here tomorrow." With so much excitement, I ran to hug her because she has help to alleviate a big stressor of mine. By the end of the night things were back on track. The food inventory had been ordered, supplies were now fully stocked, and the restaurant appeared as though it was ready to be open. If we get the part tomorrow, then we should pass the inspection and have the grand opening.

The next day when I arrived at the restaurant, I waited impatiently for the part to come. Every time I saw a delivery truck, I was at the door but after four false trips I was beginning to get worried. At noon Mason came in with a big grin on his face, not knowing that he had left. "Sis, what are you doing up here?" "I am waiting on the part to be delivered?" "That part came at nine, I signed for it and the workers have installed it. Everything is finished." Not knowing if I wanted to slap him or hug him. "Why didn't anyone tell me." "If you look at your phone you would see that I called you three hours ago" He was right, I couldn't argue with him on that one. When I went to the kitchen things appeared to be done. Now we just have made sure it is up to the inspector's approval. With two days to spare, I was just hoping that everything was okay.

When things were going well, I get this random call from Bryson and Vanessa who have been blowing my phone up all day. Finally on my way home I call them back but no answer. About twenty minutes later I get a call from my mom, when I answer for her, I then get a call from

Shynelle, so I place my mother on hold. "So, I just knew Vanessa would do something outlandish as to have a video wedding at the beach but get this she wants us to find a peach dress by tomorrow." "Wait, I am so confused. What is going on?" "Oh, let me catch you up. Your brother and his soon to be crazy wife are getting married tomorrow at the beach when the sunsets. They have the video set up for us to be her bride's maids and Mason to be one of his grooms men. Your older brothers will be there." I do a deep sigh because I knew Vanessa would do something like this, but she picked the worse timing. "I am surprised Bryson is going along with this." "Oh well he plans to do a big trip with everyone next year on their one-year anniversary and Vanessa has to go along with it apparently that is the agreement." We laughed talking about this unique but sweet wedding that we are going to be a part of tomorrow. I admit, I was excited. It gave me something else to focus on. Before I knew it, I was at the mall on the call with Shynelle and Vanessa looking for a simple but cute dress. Shynelle and I both found something similar, so we all were pleased. By the time I made it home Terrance and Mason were waiting to try to figure out how this was going to work tomorrow evening. Laughing at the confusion on their face I gave the game plan but for some reason they still seemed confused. Luckily, the photoshoot is in the morning so I will have time to set up just the way Vanessa wants us to. I was excited for my role of a virtual bridesmaid. It was fun even if it's only for a day.

Chapter 17: Cheers to Us

Everyone thinks that it was my idea to move forward with having the wedding tomorrow, but it was Bryson. I just thought it was a great idea that aligned with vison I had years ago so I was on board. I know that he may have wanted a wedding so I was going to have one but I think he knew that I didn't want to which is why he thought this would make me happy and it does. My mom didn't get as upset as I thought she would, in fact she has been distant the last few days. She seems to be madly in love with that Samuel, maybe she has just been spending more time with him. I can see them getting married in a year or so. Surprisingly, I am not against the idea of that either. Today I decided to take the day off work. Bryson also took the day off so that he could get things together such as finding a suit. He mentioned that his attire still had to be nice no matter how short notice this wedding was. I couldn't have agreed with him more on that one. I found a pretty dress a week ago when I was out shopping with my mom. She randomly took me to a gown shop, so I tried a few on. I even watched her try on a few simple gowns. It was weird at first, but I guess she was really into the moment. At the time I felt it was too early being that my intentions were to wait the typical year but luckily, I didn't. I was all set now all there was to do it get dolled up for tomorrow. I made a full pamper day for myself starting with a massage and facial.

When I arrived for my massage, I waited in the room for five minutes before the masseuse came in. She was new and I could tell because she was causing more pain than increasing relaxation. I tried not to say anything, but I just couldn't hold it in. I kindly requested another masseuse which must has happened a lot with the young lady because there was one on standby. They even gave me my ten minutes back that were wasted with the other young lady. She either needs more practice or find a new line of work but I have no idea what she was doing. I am not sure if she was using her elbow or knee but either way it was horrible. By the end of my massage, I was relaxed maneuvering to my next room to prepare for my facial. Trying to ensure they didn't send another armature I started a quick conversation asking the woman how long she has been working here. When she let me know two years, I was able to relax truly enjoying my facial. I was beyond pleased. I left the place feeling energized yet relaxed.

By the time I made it home from preparing for tomorrow, it hit me that I would be getting married. I was excited but how would that change me as a person? I have never had to check in when I wanted to go on an adventure or just take myself out on a romantic dinner. I want to have a family, but I don't want to lose myself in the process. He doesn't seem to mind but I have never brought this topic up to him. I didn't want to think about it, so I grabbed my keys to go to the store but by the time I got to the car, I remembered what I learned in counseling about facing my problems instead of running from them. Before I knew it, I was on the phone with Bryson. "Bryson, when I become your wife are you going to try to change me? I love to take trips and do things for myself things that I don't want to lose when we get married." "Those are things that I love about you; however, I don't like that you use those tactics to run from problems so that is something that we would have to work on." In the mist of our conversation, we noticed that our marriage is starting to be one of those rushed tasks that haven't been thought out. He admitted that he only wanted to do it so quickly because I told him previously that is what I wanted to do prior to us ever thinking about being in a relationship. I've since learned that marriage isn't something that should be rushed into. By the end of our conversation, we decided to hold off on tomorrow to take some time to really grow as a couple so that we could have these kinds of conversations prior to making such a big commitment. I wasn't going to lie, I was pleased. For once, I wasn't as eager to rush into something. The thought of waiting gave me a sense of relief. I wasn't sure if tomorrow that I would have gone through with it. I knew that I loved Bryson and have every intention of being his wife; however, I wanted to first be his fiancé to learn how to be his partner because I only have experience of it being just me. Taking on someone else's feelings is new to me and something that I knew I needed to work on before doing something so drastic. But because I am so used to not facing my problems, I was going to go through with something that may have resulted in nothing but a chaotic mess. He and I were both satisfied with our decision. I knew that he was only doing it to please me but honestly, I was only doing it to please him, on top of the idea of what I thought I always wanted. When he proposed I knew that this was a moment that I wanted to share with our families. The thought of not having my girls stand beside me was just ridiculous. I can't believe I thought this was a good idea and they didn't try to stop me. After we got off the phone, we decided that we would call around to let people know our change of plans. We did, however, decide that for those who were going to join us tomorrow to still host the dinner which we agreed was the least we could do for all the confusion.

When I called Shynelle and Yazmine, they were both relieved that we decided to change our minds but admitted that this was the way they always imagined me getting married. I guess I can't be mad at them for not trying to stop what I have expressed to them for years. As we were on the phone talking, we discovered that we were all discovering a new version of ourselves. It was as if we were peeling off an old layer being reintroduced to the women that we were becoming currently. It was admirable that we were all able to accept the changes that we were experiencing while empowering each other to grow as individuals. I decided not to tell my mom tonight because I just didn't have time for the lecture of why it is important that I decided to wait. I was working on facing my problems, I am just not fully vested tonight.

The next morning, I called my mom who did not answer. I wanted to leave it on her voicemail; however, that would have only created another problem. Because I had nothing to do, I went to the kitchen to make a big breakfast, something I haven't done in a very long time. I really enjoy cooking, but since its just me I don't do it much anymore. Prior to Yazmine and Shynelle leaving I would host dinner nights at my house twice a month but since they have been gone, I really hadn't cooked much. By the time I was finished I had a meal prepared for a minimum four people. I wasn't a big eater, which is why I wasn't sure what I possessed me to make so much; however, I did enjoy it. By the time I was finished I prepared to get dressed for the day. Our dinner wasn't until later tonight, therefore, I had plenty of time to spare. When I was dressed, Bryson called requesting to take me out for lunch a little later. I was still stuffed from breakfast, but I went just to spend time with him. Our lunch date rolled over into a couple of hours laughing, embracing conversation on topics that were geared towards our future together and just enjoying being in each other's presence. We were enjoying just dating one another openly and freely with no rush or expectations. We decided on marriage counseling as his parents suggested it. He was hesitant to it at first but after last night he agreed that maybe we should give it a try. So engaged in one anther it almost slipped our mind that we had plans for tonight. It also slipped my mind that I hadn't told my mom, but she still hadn't returned my call.

By the time I made it home, I changed quickly so that I could hurry to our dinner. As I grabbed my keys to leave out of the house I was met by a knock at the door. When I opened the door there was my mom dressed but with a disturbed look on her face. When I invited her in, she declined just requesting to ride to the place with me. I was puzzled as to what was happening. I wasn't sure if she had heard from Bryson's parents that we decided to wait and now she is upset with me, but I didn't have time to wait for one of her big teachable moments so when we got in the car I asked. "Mom, what's wrong? I am sorry if you found out from someone else that we decided to hold off on getting married, but I tried to call you this morning." Still, she didn't say anything, but she did seem shocked about the news as if she wasn't aware of this change of plans. All of which had me just a tad bit more confused than before. At this point I was over it, so I pulled into the nearest gas station parked requesting my mom say whatever it is that has her acting so strange. "So, what is it mom, why are you acting so strange." For five minutes she didn't say a word, but I refused to leave until she spoke. "Vanessa…" waiting for her to say the rest I look over at my mom who is holding her hand that now has an engagement ring on it. "Oh shit, I mean oh wow congratulations mom. Is tonight cheers to us? When did he propose to you?" I said a mouthful as I was reaching over in attempt to give my mother a hug as she hesitated yet again. "Well…" "Mom, I have never seen you this quiet so what's up speak woman." "Vanessa, I am married. We got married a week ago, but I was so ashamed that I rushed off to do it without you that I just didn't know how to tell you. Then when you decided to have a rushed wedding still including me, I felt completely horrible. I am extremely sorry baby it was just one of those things that we just both knew we wanted." Stunned by what my mom just revealed to me; I wasn't sure if I were hurt by her not including me or just stunned that she had it in her to just live freely for once. I knew that she has been happy but for her to just jump into a marriage so quickly was so out of character. I was hoping it was all due to love and not because the fear of getting older or that freak accident, she had a while back. Either way, I was still upset that it took her a week to tell me. As I was driving, she continued to apologize and tried to show me pictures. The thing that took me over the edge was that he had his daughter there as a witness. "Look Vanessa, I just have preached to you your entire life about making logical decisions that in this instance I knew you wouldn't believe that I had truly thought things threw. I just knew you wouldn't be able to understand because I haven't never tried to understand your impulsive behavior, but this is different. I really thought about it before going forward." "So, even after all that thinking you didn't think to include me?" There was silence for the next twenty minutes. I have never been able to silence my mother, ever. She knew she was wrong. I stopped being hurt that she waited so long to tell me. However, I was emotionally wounded and in a state of disbelief that she didn't give me the opportunity to be a part of something so life changing. It has always been the two of us and in this situation, she chose not to have me a part of it which hurt. When I found out that his daughter was there as the witness, I felt myself close into a shell.

When I made it to the beachside restaurant it was supposed to be a joyous occasion; however, I couldn't hide the hurt that I was feeling. It was displayed on my face and in my actions. When Samuel and his daughter tried to approach me, I walked off leaving them right where they stood. I was hurt so I wanted them to know how it felt. Bryson approached me so I filled him in on what was going on. He tried to convince me to talk with my mother so that we could enjoy our night, but I just wanted to get away. Before I knew it, I had snuck away preparing to walk on the beach when I heard someone "running away bride!" When I turned around it was Shynelle. "What are you doing here?" "Well, I couldn't let you get married without at least one of us. I got my ticket before you let us know that you changed your mind, so I decided to still come. What is wrong with you Vanessa? Everyone is in there to celebrate you and Bryson, yet you are out here." "My mom has run off and gotten married but get this she didn't include me. No, she included her new daughter." "I get you're upset, but what is walking on the beach doing for you right now? You have a fiancé in there upset that you are choosing to let something that can be addressed later upset what he is spending his hard-earned money on to celebrate the two of you. Sometimes, you must learn to let things go so that you can live in the moment of right now. You can't control every aspect of your life no matter how badly you want to. That will cause you more pain than you know it. Try living in the present moment for once, no distraction or in your case adventures so you call it. Just live in the moment and see how much life changes for you." I had to admit, she was right. Being in control of things has continuously kept me on the go as if I have been running from what is right in front of me. I hated to admit it but that is exactly what it is. "What would I do without you?" "Hell, I don't know. Probably run to New Mexico." We laughed all the way back to the restaurant where I was met by an upset Bryson who gave me the cold shoulder for two seconds. That is until I apologized begging for his forgiveness.

We gathered amongst some family and friends taking time to celebrate a new phase in our lives that were preparing to enter. It was a happy occasion for the two of us which made me even more excited about the future to come. I had a lot of growing and learning to do so that I could enter a new phase with the man of my dreams. It was beautiful. Yazmine did a video call that only she could pull off. Her speech made us laugh yet cry all at the same time. It was magical, something that I had never imagined but something that I have always longed for.

The following day I was able to meet with my mother to discuss the issue that I allowed to take precedence over Bryson and I engagement dinner. Our conversation allowed me to accept that both of our lives were changing. However, we agreed to continue to make efforts to include each other in life changing moments going forward. I was still upset about what she had done but I was trying to move forward dealing with what was presently in front of me. It was hard; however, I managed. I even took it a little further to apologize to Samuel and his daughter, but it was evident that it was not genuine, but I didn't care. When my mother invited me to stay for dinner, I declined saying that I had plans, but she knew that I wasn't telling the truth.

When I left, I didn't have anything to do plus I was hungry. I reached out to Bryson to meet for dinner. He decided to meet at our favorite Italian restaurant. Once we finished, we decided to shop for some shoes to go with the outfits that we had for Yazmine grand opening. We searched shortly but there was nothing that caught our eyes, so we decided to order something online later that night. Because we were by the movie theater, we decided to go see whatever was playing. That was a bad idea. We sat in a theater filled with teens walking back and forth not to mention talking loudly; just ridiculous. We couldn't enjoy the movie, so we decided to leave. "Are we the old people who complain at the movies now?" (both laughing) "I guess, because it took everything in me not to take ole boy and make his ass sit down. I mean damn, it was apparent that he was macking two girls, he should have just sat them together at this point." "That's how you were when I met you." "Yeah, but I had more game. I would have never taken two of my ladies out at the same time, that's just a disaster waiting to unfold." "Good thing you got your whorish ways out before we started dating." "Oh, I would have been done if you had given me a chance back in the day." "…and we both know that not to be true." We continued to talk until we arrived at my car. "Honestly, I've known since the day that I met you that you were the one worth changing for. Never thought I would be blessed with the opportunity to date you but when the opportunity presented itself, I had to show up as the man you needed. I can't wait until the day I get to call you my wife and you have my big-headed babies." Blushing as he opened my car door kissing me as if we were not both heading to his house. As I followed Bryson to his place, it became apparent to me that my life was evolving in a good way; one that didn't frighten me but made me want to sit still in the moment.

Chapter 18: Inspector

The morning of the photoshoot, I was running behind because I just kept forgetting things. Mason had gone on ahead of me which worked in my favor because they were able to get him started without me. By the time I arrived he was just beginning his first shot. I got my hair touched up; makeup done then I got dressed. I took a few shots, then Mason joined me for a few. The unedited photos were gorgeous so I can only imagine how amazing the final edits will be. I was proud of my brother stepping out living his dream. I was happy that I could help to make it happen. Once we finished, Mason had the idea to pass out samples of two of the menu items on the beach along with flyers to advertise the grand opening. I changed into something a little more comfortable but still cute. Mason put on another chef coat then we headed to the beach where we were met with Nyla and two of the other staff that started this week. He sampled some Cajun lobster rolls and Caribbean pineapple chicken wings, and it was a hit. I am not sure if it were just the food or the ladies love for my brother, but they were invested in ensuring to be at the grand opening and thereafter. There was even an older woman obsessed with my brother that I thought I was going to have to get a water hose for her. I heard many great reviews about the food making them excited to see what else is on the menu. I was pleased with such great feedback. This afternoon we had an interview with a few bartenders that are coming up with specialty drinks. I have an idea of the young lady that I want but I plan to give everyone a fair opportunity because sometimes I am surprised at how talented these younger people are. I mean Mason and Nyla put together this tasting to promote the grand opening which was a great idea. I am ecstatic that I finally have a phenomenal team on my side. With the tasting coming to an end, we finished up to get to the restaurant for the second-round interview which is for the bartenders to show their skill set behind the bar.

Upon arrival to the restaurant, the four interviewees were there waiting with their tools. Terrance pulled up shortly after we arrived. In the interview it was Terrance, Mason, Nyla, and me. The four bartenders set up behind the bar as they went down the line starting with the young lady from New York. Her presentation was fantastic; however, her drink was nothing magical. The second lady seemed to just decide to bartend this moment because she had no clue as to what she was doing. The third guy was well experienced, and his drink was great. The young lady that I was rooting for had a great drink, but her presentation was in dire need of work. After discussing we decided on hiring the man as the lead bartender and the first and fourth lady as the two additional. That was the final interview selection that I had to complete for the restaurant so now all there was to do is prepare to for opening night. We did a final walk through of the kitchen to ensure we had everything needed for opening night, food, utensils, cleaning supply and so on. Things were great, well organized, and ready for the big day.

With only two weeks left until opening night, the getters were still settling in. Not to mention, I still had to deal with the inspector on tomorrow. Just hoping he is not an asshole so that we can continue to move forward with things. When everyone left, I did a final walk through to make sure that everything was in place, tidy for the inspection in the morning. The inspector said he would be here at 7:15, an awkward time just already doing the most, but I know his ass will get here promptly at 7am so I plan to be here waiting on him. After I complete my walk through, I lock the doors to get home for the night. Terrance and Mason had gone to the gym for a game of basketball by the time I arrived home, so I sat on my computer working on the schedule for opening night. Not too many people had special request which made it a bit easier to create the schedule unlike before. I had a tentative schedule created with backups just in case people have a change of mind when I call them tomorrow giving them their official start date. When I finalized my work for the night, I walk to the kitchen to get something to eat when I remembered that I had to call for the engagement dinner. I called giving what was supposed to be a simple congratulations which turned into a speech because I was so happy for my brother finding his soulmate in one of my best friends. I got kind of emotional, but I tried not to show it as much. By the time I was ending the call with them, Terrance, and Mason walk in appearing to have hit a bar on their route home. Before I knew it the music was playing, we had wings, and a card game happening on the deck. As we were playing, Terrance notices our neighbor peep out his back door, but I guess he didn't have anything to say tonight so he didn't come out. After winning three rounds of cards, I was ready to call it a night, so I went to bed leaving them up playing pool. Nervous about tomorrow, I wanted to be sure to get enough sleep so that I could be alert and present during the walk through in the morning. The contractor is a cool guy who confirmed that he would be there just in case there are some things that the inspector says need to be done. He is a friend of my husband, so he really wants things to go as planned for us. I was truly grateful.

The next morning, the damn inspector really tried to run some bullshit game on me. That morning he was at the door at 7 am promptly. As I intended on him doing so, I was there waiting for him. He wore these brown glasses that appeared to haven't been cleaned in months, how he could see out of them was surprising to me. He had to be all of 4' 11" tall, wearing a brown pinstripe suit, old brief case with this permanent frown on his face. I have worked with him previously and there hasn't been one time that I have seen him smile. When he walked in, he immediately goes to the kitchen checking for the missing piece. After about ten minutes trying to create a problem with it, he finally gave it a pass. Just when I thought he was done he started to walk around to all the places that he given a pass to on the previous visit. Just as he was finishing grabbing his clip board, I notice him take a step back towards the freezer. He walked in but couldn't find anything wrong, so I thought then he but out "this is the incorrect temperature gage for this freezer." Before I could cuss this short man out the contractor was there with the correct gage, which was a quick fix, resulting in a passed inspection. By the end the older gentleman passed me the report smiling letting me know that this place looks great. I was almost willing to extend an invite until he tossed the paper on the counter instead of passing it to me in my had. I kindly escorted the older gentleman out of my building so that he could get to harassing whoever else is on his list today. I was overjoyed with excitement to be done with him but mostly to move forward with getting this place up and running.

By nine, Nyla had arrived ready to assist with calling the other staff about their official first day. The soft opening will be some of the staff's first night; however, we have a two-day training next week. To my surprise, we didn't have to make any adjustments as everyone was on board for the start day including the two-day training that they had already been previewed to. It was noon and everything was set. Watching everything come together was quite satisfying. After I finished up at the restaurant, I had just enough time to start this yoga class. When I got to the class, I was rusty being that I hadn't been in over a year, but I feel as though I don't need to take a beginner's class. After we started of I immediately regrated my decision. Luckily, the instructor remembered me from attending previously so she gave me a tremendous amount of help until I got back into the swing of things. By the end of the class, I was intermediate level, feeling like a baddie walking out of the class having fallen over six of the twelve poses that we did. Oh, but I was still walking out confident as if I knew what the heck, I were doing letting them know that I'd be back tomorrow with no real intention to be at this class.

When I made it to the car, I called Shynelle immediately letting her know how embarrassed I was. In trying to do the bound lizard yoga pose when I fell over hitting the young lady next to me. I apologized and she accepted but I think by the second hit she was over it which is why she moved over to the other side of the class. I didn't care though; I had paid my money for the class just has she had done so I stayed trying to endeavor each pose the instructor demonstrated. I was not prepared for the advanced class. Shynelle didn't answer so as I was sitting there, I went on the site to change my classes from advanced to beginners with the same instructor because I really enjoy her classes; however, I wasn't ready for those high-level classes just yet. As I was pulling out of the parking lot, I received a call from Terrance letting me know that he had something special for the two of us requesting that I pack an overnight bag and be prepared to leave once he gets off work. I was excited. I love his surprises; I mean his last surprise was me hanging with my girl Shynelle so I could only imagine what he has planned for us now. I didn't have plans for the next two days other than getting the training material ready for next week which only requires some tweaks. Mason has sent over his portion of training, and I can tell that we had the same parents. His work was flawless. Our parents did not play when it came to things like that. We were always told "if you're going to put your name on something, make sure it is always your best work." Well, it finally stuck with us, I mean we got tired of phones, laptops just fun in general being taken away from us so they finally got through to us. Mason was made for this. I couldn't wait to see him in action in a few weeks. Listening to all his aspirations inspired me. When I was his age, I had no clue as to what I wanted to do which is why I dropped out of college to do real-estate. I just so happened to like real estate making it work for me.

When I arrived home, there was a car parked outside my home which I didn't recognize. When I opened the garage, to my surprise Terrance was already home. When I walked in "hey who car is that outside"? "mine", I heard Mason say as he was walking from the back. "Oh shit, that is nice so that is what you have been saving for? I am proud of you." "Yeah, besides riding a bike isn't the life of the new head chef." I was extremely proud of him; unlike my other brothers he too didn't spend his money on new flashy cars. He saved, working hard so that when the time was right, he could get what he truly wanted. He drove my old car back home which held up quite nicely, but it was time for him to get some new wheels. And he did just that. He promised to take me for a ride as soon as I returned home from my getaway. Terrance was ready having already packed a bag for me. I wasn't so sure about that, but I didn't put up a fight.

We were in the car for a short period before we arrived at this resort. We check into our room then go to this beautiful restaurant. The night was simple and sweet. "Yazmine, I know I said I wouldn't do this again, but an opportunity has presented itself that I believe would be great for our family." "Okay, so now I see the motive behind the surprise trip." "No, not exactly. I have had this information for a while now I just thought it would be the best time to tell you. I have been offered a job in Arizona that aligns with everything that I have been working so hard for." "What about what I have been working hard for?" "Baby, you can do it again there." "Then when you get another grand job opportunity am I supposed to just jump at your command." "I get it, I have asked you to do this before, but I've been working my ass off to be the chief executive and you know that." "I do, but I left a career that I enjoyed moving here with you starting over from scratch and just as things are going well you want me to just stop?" "I want you to consider what this opportunity could do for the both of us. I have always supported you. I'd even promise to make sure that your restaurant here still thrives. I'd make sure that all your work isn't in vain, I just can't do this without your support. Please think about it. We would be closer to family and Shynelle lives there too. I believe your restaurant is in good hands with Mason and Nyla. That way you could have your restaurant then get back into developing your rental properties. Just think about it. I have a few weeks to give an answer." I was sitting across from this man that I love but really didn't like in the moment. I had so many thoughts racing through my mind that I really didn't enjoy dinner. That night in the room, we really didn't talk. He worked for a while and so did I.

The next morning as I was getting dressed, he asked me to join him for the couple massage that he had planned. Hesitantly I went along. The walk to the place was quiet. I could see that he wanted me to say something, but I had no words to say. On one hand I wanted to support my husband as I have but then I also wanted him to stay here to support me. I wanted to see the success of this place that I have invested so much time and energy into. I have grown to love running my own restaurant it gave me a sense of pride, I would think that he knew that. I was stuck between choosing between my husband and my career which isn't a great space to be in. When we arrived at the room we were greeted with drinks, snacks and two masseuses. "Baby, don't think about anything right now, just relax you deserve it." Terrance said as he leaned over to give me a kiss. I put a slight smile on my face as the masseuse began our foot massage. It was so soothing that I went to sleep. By the time they were finished it was time for us to get our back massages. We were in a room so relaxing with the lights dimmed. He was lying on the table beside me. Again, about five minutes into the massage, I fell asleep. When I got up Terrance was sitting waiting for me as I had been sleeping for a little longer than the massage lasted. Luckily, there wasn't another booking, so they allowed us to keep the room. When I gathered myself, we got dressed preparing to leave. Again, silent the entire trip. I could tell that he was getting agitated, but he didn't say anything. I still had no words. I didn't want to make an impulsive decision. "Terrance, I have been thinking about what we talked about last night, but I still don't have a clue as to what I think would be best. If you would allow me some more time to think I would appreciate it." "That is all that I can ask of you baby, thank you for even considering it. I would love for us to stay here so when they approached me about the position, I was thrilled thinking it was here but when they said I would have to relocate again, I was bummed." "I understand, we will figure it out." He smiled at me as he continued to drive us home. When we got home, Mason had cleared his things out of the house. He called earlier letting me know that he had finally moved out. I was aware of him looking for a place, but I didn't know the move would happen so fast. He asked me to give him a call when I made it, so I did. He invited us over to see his new place. Terrance had work to catch up on, so he declined until a later date. I however, jumped in my car driving to Mason's place. When I arrived, it was a beautiful apartment walking distance from the beach and shopping centers. It was beautiful the perfect size for him. It was empty however, so after he gave me a tour, I decided to take him shopping for some things for his place. He had never lived on his own, so it was exciting for the both of us. When we arrived at the store, we got the essentials like food, cleaning supplies towels, blow up mattress and sheets. Later, we unpacked the things that we had gotten on our mini shopping spree; then I helped him clean. Once we were finished, we ordered pizza and watched tv on the only piece of furniture that he has. We made plans to look at furniture in the morning. I offered to give him one of the guest bedrooms set but he wanted to see what he could find first. After the movie went off, I helped Mason with his blow-up mattress then I left for home. When I arrived, Terrance was sleep so I sat on the deck thinking about what the best option would be. I sat there for about an hour before I had fallen asleep. I was awakened by a damn lizard crawling up my leg. I screamed so loudly that I am sure I woke the entire neighborhood. Terrance came running to find me making sure I was okay. Then there was a loud "shut up" out of nowhere. When we looked it was the old man next door in his bathrobe on his deck yelling for me to be quiet. He is the sweetest grouch I have ever met. He will cook for you then kick you out right after. We both looked at one another laughing as we walked into the house.

The next morning, I was leaving the house for yoga class when I was stopped by the old man from last night who was flagging me down. I stopped, rolling down my window as he slowly walked down his driveway in the same bathrobe sipping on his morning cup of coffee "Darling, I am so sorry that I yelled at you last night, but you scared the dog shit out of me." "Oh, it is perfectly fine. I apologize for scaring you." "It's fine darling, just don't do it again." He patted me on the shoulder as he reached in his robe pocket passing me a small grocery list that he asked me to pick up for him while I was out today. I graciously grabbed the list and headed on my way. Yoga class was amazing, I didn't fall at all and the members attitude were pleasing. When I left, I stopped by the store to grab the items on the list. When I called my neighbor to let him know that they didn't have the brand of coffee he listed he insisted that I was wrong. Being that I didn't want to argue with him this morning I went to the store across the street.

Luckily, this store had it, so I dropped the items off to him and he took the bag looking into them. "Thank you darling, see I told you didn't look good enough. I knew that they had my coffee." I clearly passed him two different store bags but again, I just let him be right as he walked slowly back towards his home.

When I was all refreshed from my shower, I got dressed so that I could meet Mason at the furniture store. As we arrived to the store, the salesman was super pushy and the items were just not what Mason wanted so we tried another store. When we arrived at the next store the sales associate was very helpful to find the right pieces to suit Mason style. He found a nice affordable bedroom set and living room set. My parents purchased him a dining room set since he loves to host. Mason was over shopping but allowed me to take him to a few additional stores just to buy him some accessories to add character to his home. After we finished, we sat for a late lunch talking about the opening of the restaurant when we both received an email of the photos from our photoshoot. They exceeded our expectations. We decided on the ones that we wanted displayed in the restaurant. We then ended our lunch taking Mason's things home so that he could go play a game of basketball. I decided to go to the beach to finish reading my book which was a great idea. It gave me time to think, reflect, and just relax. I concluded on what would be best for Terrance and me so I will discuss it with him tonight.

Chapter 19: Sandwich Shop

After romantic trips and unexpected non-wedding dinners, I was finally back in the swing of work focusing on me. I had missed a few sessions at the gym, which I felt when I got back in there. My trainer made it her business to make sure to give me extra sets for skipping a few times. I was beyond tired when I left the gym this afternoon. I went to the grocery store to pick up some food for the week since I hadn't had time to shop in a while. Eating out was making me lethargic. I can see the difference in my body when I don't eat right or exercise which is why I am getting back to focusing on me. I have a boxing class with Lisa tomorrow. I haven't told her about Ken just yet. I want to keep that to myself for a little while longer just to see how things play out between us. She tends to overshare everyone's business and I don't want this to be out just yet until I am sure about him. When I arrive to the store, it was so packed that I almost decided to ditch the idea of grocery shopping to grab some food, but I decided against it. When I got into the store it wasn't as busy as I thought. I grabbed the items that I needed for the week then proceeded to check out. When I was in line there was a handsome gentleman who tried to give me his number but I declined, he still gave me his card that was for a construction company which was apparent that he worked for from the attire that he had on. But even through the dirty clothes, he was still handsome. In my entire existence there have never been so many men to approach me and today I don't even feel I look my best. I still have on my gym set from working out. I took the card not to cause a scene putting it in my purse walking away as I leave out the store. When I make it to my car putting my items in the trunk the gentleman from the store says, "I hope to hear from you gorgeous" as he waves goodbye walking to his car. I was flattered to be noticed but I had not intentions on calling him because I wanted to see how it works out with Ken who really does have trust issues, which reminded me to toss his card out of my purse.

When I arrive home, there is a package at my door. I grab it, then put my things away. Once I was finished, I hurry to jump in the shower. When I get out the shower wearing my favorite yellow robe that Vanessa bought me with the matching slippers, I sit on the couch to open the package. It was an elegant rustic sleeveless lace tulle, ruffles with a high split evening gown that I showed Ken that I was thinking about getting for Yazmine grand opening. I had no clue that he was really paying attention as we were both sitting at the table working at the time. He really paid attention to detail, one of the many traits that I liked about him. I picked up the phone to give him a call, but I knew he would be working late so I expected to go to voicemail but to my surprise he answered on the first ring. "Hello Shynelle" "Hi Ken, I was expecting to get your voicemail. I just wanted to thank you for the beautiful dress." "Of course, I'd answer for you. And you're welcome, is that the right one?" "It is." "I wasn't sure, when you were telling me I heard you a little, so I had to grab your computer when you stepped away to get some water hoping that I got the right information to get it for you." "Well, you did. Thank you." He and I talked for a short period before he had to finish up work. I was learning to have more of a work life balance which has been working out pleasantly. However, there are some nights that I still find myself working late, it's just not as consuming as before for now.

Later that night, I gave Mason a call so that he could assist me in making a meal that I saw on one of his videos. He graciously helped and it was delicious. When I was about finished cooking, Ken stopped by to surprise me with some flowers. We sat down ate dinner together, talking the night away. The next morning, we had breakfast before leaving out for work. When I arrived at work, I was met by Lisa. "Are we still on for boxing tonight?" "Definitely." I continued to my office preparing for the workday that turned out to be the usual amount of busy. As the workday was coming to an end Lisa barges in my office requesting that I hurry up.

When we arrive to class, the instructor didn't waste any time to start. By the end of the class, Lisa and I were both drenched in sweat. My legs and arms felt like jelly. We found ourselves holding each other up to get out of the class. As I was preparing to depart, Lisa insisted that I join her for dinner. I wanted nothing more than to take a bubble bath and sit on my couch in my robe, but she wasn't taking no for an answer.

We ended up at the small sandwich shop next door. I wasn't that hungry, so I just got a smoothie. As we were waiting for our ordered to be prepared Lisa's husband and Nathan walk in, immediately sitting at the table with us. I made it clear to Lisa and Nathan that I didn't have an interest in him so why they are here baffles me. As I was gathering my things out of all people in walks Ken who walks over to speak. As I introduce him Nathan speaks as if to insinuate that we were being interrupted on a date which made Ken look at me with utter disgust. I try to walk over to him to explain but as he stated from the beginning, he has a no tolerance for playing games. I was in a crazy predicament that I didn't even do. When Ken walked out, I immediately walked over to the table. "Lisa, I have made it very clear to you that I don't need your help dating. I am perfectly happy. And Nathan if I hadn't made it clear to you. You and I will never be. Sorry but not sorry." Before anyone could utter a word, I grabbed my purse to leave.

On my ride home I felt so bad. It wasn't just a relationship I was building with Ken that I had unintentionally ruined, there is my special bond with Mr. and Mrs. Thompson. I was so lost and confused. I tried to call Ken, but he didn't answer. I even made a trip to his home, but he wasn't there. I didn't want to get Mr. and Mrs. Thompson involved so I decided to go home. I called Yazmine so that she could give me some advice. She basically told me to allow him to calm down then try to talk it out with him because clearly there is a misunderstanding. I wanted so badly for her to be right; I was experiencing a new type of happiness that I wasn't ready to let go of and all because Lisa doesn't know how to respect my wishes. I must make my boundaries clear and precise with her when it pertains to my dating life. When I arrived home, Lisa called to apologize again, I let her know not to do it again and she understood ensuring to respect my wishes from now on. After I showered, I checked my phone yet still no call from Ken, so I browsed the tv for something to watch. Yazmine called to see if I had heard anything, but I hadn't so she talked to me for a short period trying to be a distraction. It worked for the time being but when the call ended, I tried to call again. When I went to sleep that night, I had come to the realization that I hadn't done anything wrong, I tried to communicate with him to explain the situation so if he doesn't return my call by tomorrow, I will just have to accept that and move on.

The next morning, I woke up headed to the gym. After my workout I went home, showered, got dressed and had some breakfast. I had gone the entire morning without checking my phone in hopes that he would have reached out. When I pulled up at work before going in, I checked my phone but still no call nor text. So, in that moment I kept my word, and I didn't try to reach out again. The following week I gave Lisa the cold shoulder but that wasn't my character, and I didn't like treating her like that, so I pulled her to the side apologizing letting her know the situation. Even after giving her the cold shoulder, she was still so apologetic making me feel even worse. As I was leaving the office that night, I saw Mr. Thompson who was getting off the elevator and there was no way of avoiding him. "Hey lil bit, I haven't heard from you in a while. I hope everything is okay." "Hi, Mr. Thompson, everything is fine, just busy working. How are you and Mrs. Thompson?" "We are doing well. Mrs. Thompson is taking it easy ever since her accident that hip of hers keeps giving her issues but overall, we can't complain. I hope to see you over soon." He gives me a big hug and I help him walk his things to the car. He didn't mention Ken at all, so I guess he hadn't said anything to them. With all that has been going on I only had a few days before I must get to Yazmine grand opening remembering that I needed shoes to go with my dress. So, with no plans I go on a mini shopping spree. In the first store I was lucky enough to find the perfect pair of shoes that would accentuate the evening gown perfectly. I was pleased, deciding to treat myself to a nice dinner at this new French restaurant nearby. When I got there, I decided to sit at a table being that it wasn't as crowed as I anticipated. I ordered a nice glass of wine as I looked over the menu. After reviewing the menu for a short period of time I hear in a deep tone. "I sure was waiting on that call". When I look up it was the gentleman from the grocery store standing in front of me now wearing a blue suit, nicely fitted with a tie, nicely groomed bald head and a shiny moisturized beard. I didn't have the words to say because I didn't know how to say kindly that I threw your card out. "It's, okay I just saw you from across the room and I couldn't resist not to speak to the beautiful woman from the grocery store." He made me smile. "I'm sorry. I honestly didn't have intentions of calling you I just didn't know how to let you down in the store." He smiled "I understand, I will not hold you up any longer I just wanted to say hello. Enjoy your dinner." He smiled at me as he walked away. "Shynelle" "Excuse me?"

"My name is Shynelle" "Well enjoy your dinner Ms. Shynelle." For some reason I was smiling harder than a smiley face emoji. I watched him as he went across the restaurant where he appeared to be having a meeting with some other gentlemen. That evening I glanced over to his side of the restaurant a few times during my meal trying not to be obvious. Right before I was finished with my meal, I glanced over his way again; however, this time the table had been cleared. I am not sure why but a part of me wanted him to give me his number again. I sat for a second longer deciding if I wanted to order dessert, deciding against it I request my check but was informed that my bill had been paid by the gentleman at the bar. When I looked over there, he was sitting at the bar, so I went over to thank him. Before long I was sitting with Naeem who owns the contracting company that was displayed on the business card that he provided a while back at the grocery store. He has been divorced for a few years with no kids. He surprised me with how good of a time I had with just sitting talking with him. We talked for about an hour, by the end of the night I requested that we exchange numbers. I wasn't sure if I were going to use it but for someone who has never really dated it felt good to date to just see what is out there. On my way home I called Yazmine to tell her about this situation. Our conversation lasted until I arrived home. She basically liked the idea of me dating to see what I really want. Although she believes Ken seemed to be an okay guy, his lack of communication when an issue arises and the red flags in his behavior when it comes to trust is something that can be detrimental to a lasting relationship which I could not agree with more. Our conversation really had me thinking, was I overlooking his extreme behaviors due to him polishing it up with extreme gestures. By the time I had made it home Vanessa called sharing her experience in couples counseling, sounding like a little cursing therapist herself.

When I finished up the call with my friends, I ran me a nice relaxing bubble bath, got a glass of wine and played some soft jazz music to relax. When I got out of the tub, I just was in a mood to pamper myself, so I did a facial. Once I was finished, I put on my favorite pajamas then cut on a scary movie as I finished my glass of wine. I wasn't tired but I decided to call it a night. Just as I was cutting my lamp off, I received a call from Mrs. Thompson saying that Mr. Thompson had been unresponsive, so she was in the ambulance with him on the way to the hospital. She didn't need to say anything else before I could get my thoughts together, I had on a pair of work out pants, shirt, and the slides I had sitting near my front door. I am not sure if I matched or how I appeared I just knew that Mrs. Thompson needed me, so I was going to be there. When I arrived at the hospital, I found Mrs. Thompson who was calm, but I could feel her panicking as I held her hand. After hours of waiting the doctors let us know that his blood was low causing him to be unresponsive. The doctor thinks that it is time for him to start stepping away from the heavy load of trying to work and just relax. Mr. Thompson isn't going to like that one bit. When we waked in the room, I helped Mrs. Thompson over to her husband who was thrilled to see her after this traumatic ordeal. I stayed with them all night that night. At about 3 in the morning, I left for my gym session making it on time looking a mess. Then I went home to prepare for the workday. By the end of the day, I had received a missed call from Ken who now wants to talk. I had the urge to see what he wanted but I didn't call. After work I grabbed a few things form Mr. and Mrs. Thompson from their house then dropped if off at the hospital. That is when I learned that Ken has been gone for a business trip which is why they were so grateful to have me show up for them as I did last night and have in the past. It was apparent that they knew that something was going on between he and I, but they didn't try to pressure me to find out. I sat we them for a little while longer then left to go home. As I was leaving out, Mrs. Thomas walks out the room with me grabbing my hand thanking me for me for always being there for them. As I was about to reply, she grabs my hand tighter "you are a lot to everyone else, don't forget to do the same for yourself. You deserve every bit of happiness that God has in store for you so don't settle for anything less than what you deserve no matter who it is." She winked at me giving me a kiss on the cheek before she walked back in the room with her husband. I am not sure what she meant by that, but it really weighed heavy on my heart during my ride home.

Later that evening I tried to call Ken back, but it continued to send me to voicemail. I didn't leave a message because I didn't know what to say. I hated that I had to leave Mr. and Mrs. Thompson alone but I did plan for them a ride home tomorrow and gave them Lisa number if they needed anything before Ken returns. I was preparing to leave tomorrow immediately after work to get in town a day before Yazmine's two-day event. Had it been any other situation I would have been late, but I couldn't miss this, and they understood.

Chapter 20: Encore

Still not on the best of terms with my mother, we all prepared to leave for Yazmine's event. I had no clue that we would all be on the same flight. On top of that, I was forced to sit behind my mom, her new husband and daughter. I don't even understand why she is coming; I mean doesn't she have a final or something. I didn't make a scene because I promised Bryson, I would have a good time. When we arrived, my mother didn't seem to be bothered that she and I hadn't talked as much. I just knew for sure that she would have tried to do lunch or something by now, but she hasn't. When we were grabbing our bags, she gave me a slight hug, but I have to admit, I was jealous. Instead of me getting a father figure, I felt like I was losing the one person that I have had all this time. I couldn't let this fester on any longer. When we were walking to our next terminal, I grabbed my mom impulsively to have a conversation that I felt couldn't wait. "Mom, I feel like I am losing you and I need you now more than ever." "Baby you will forever be my everything and there is nothing nor anyone that could ever destroy the bond that we have. I am sorry for not including you in such a big life changing decision. I was just embarrassed that for years I have been wanting you to think things through that I made an impulsive decision that just luckily worked out for me. Believe me when I say, you aren't losing me you just gaining a better, happier version of me." I hug her with a sense of peace because those were just the words that I needed hear. My counselor told me for weeks to try talking with her but stubbornly I avoided doing so. I felt better. I was even able to talk to Samuel and his daughter who came along to spend time with her dad before she starts law school. She and I have so much in common and she is truly a great girl. Once I let go of the anger, I was able to see that again. When she said she is happy to have a big sister it made me smile because I have always wanted to have that type of relationship. It was like everything was starting to align perfectly for me. I was learning to let go of things that were out of my control living in the moment, addressing things that bother me, happy in a relationship that brings me peace and a family to call my own. It was time for me to embrace the changes that are happening in my life.

This trip to see Yazmine was already starting off on the right track. Bryson and I were showing up together, thank goodness.

When we arrived Bryson and I were able to check in early because our room was ready; however, everyone else had to wait so we put their luggage in our room so that we could sightsee. Yazmine was completing her additional training with staff who seemed to need a tad bit more help, so she planned to meet us a little later. We all decided to go to the beach just to get out of the hotel, somehow, we ended up at the bar because when on vacation why not. I watched my reserved mother get on stage with her husband to do karaoke and it was hilarious however embarrassing. Then she had the audacity to shout me out letting everyone know that the crazy lady singing was my mother. Bryson made it no better being that he went up there afterwards, although he could sing, I just wanted them to sit down. When they didn't, I figured just cheer them on so that evening I was at a family concert enjoying every bit of it. By the time Yazmine walked in on her natural high Bryson pulled her up on stage so that could do a duet. Without hesitation she joined him. They were so entertaining that people started crowding around the stage as if they were at true concert. I even saw one couple get up to dance. When they were getting off stage the crowed screamed "encore" hyping them to do one more song. Once they were finished the bartender had a round of shots for everyone in our group of people which included Mason, Terrance, and Yazmine's parents who had now joined the party. It was a pleasantly good time bringing back the memories that we had together prior to everyone moving away. It was just what everyone needed. I sent Shynelle a video making her pissed that she couldn't get an earlier flight because she loves karaoke. We had plans to hang out tonight when she arrived. She is staying with Yazmine, so we all plan to check out the Miami night life.

About two hours later we decided to get back to the hotel so that everyone else could check into their rooms. We arrived just in time because we were having so much fun that we almost forgot. In the room I laid on the bed resting being that Bryson went with Yazmine to hang out for a while longer. I planned to meet with them later allowing them time with each other because in talking to him on the flight I could see how much he missed his sister. I couldn't rest so I flipped through the channels, but it was something about being on vacation and sitting in the room that just did not sit well with me. I called Noelle, Samuel's daughter to see what she was doing. We decided to put on our bathing suites and head to the beach. The sun was shining bright, and the sand was warm between our toes. On the beach was a bar we went to both ordering long islands. We found a chair on the beach, opened the umbrella preparing to lay out when the waitress came over to take our order both ordering wings. The sun felt good against my skin, this beat laying in the bed in the hotel. The birds were swarming, and kids were playing. There was one kid who buried his mom in the sand then walked off laughing when she told him to help her out. I tried not to laugh but when Noelle laughed, I couldn't resist. Her husband was so preoccupied in his phone that he didn't hear her when she called out for him, so we decided to help her out. I think the kid regretted his decision because she was so upset, she made her family get up and leave the beach. I felt bad for his sister because she was being punished for his mischievous behavior. "That kind of stuff makes me glad that I didn't have a sibling" Noelle said. "Yeah, that would have pissed me off but when they get older, she will be able to reminisce on that ass whooping that he is about to get in the car" I said pointing as I saw the mom grab him up to head to the car. We were both now sitting there laughing enjoying the simplicity of nature's beautiful art. Our food arrived so we ate. Just as we were finishing it began to rain extremely hard out of nowhere, so we rushed back to the hotel. By the time we finally made it to the hotel we were drenched in rainwater. Once in the hotel the rain stopped. We didn't want to get back out there so we decided to go back to our rooms to change.

After getting out the shower Yazmine sent me a video of her and Bryson on some scooters. It was evident that the two of them had no clue of what they were doing because he fell but quickly got back on as if it never happened. They were having a blast. We still had plenty of time before we had to meet up later so when my mother asked me to join them on their trip to the mall, I was all for it. It was different being the four of us but in a good way. At the mall, Noelle and I ventured off to do our own thing then met back up with our parents about an hour later. She was fun and a tad bit spontaneity in the sense that she wasn't afraid to try new things, something that I liked. By the end of our shopping excursion, we went for a walk to sightsee just to pass time until it was time for everyone to depart to go do their own separate things. The parents had plans to go to this jazz spot later tonight where the younger people plan to hang out at Yazmine house then this beachside club.

Chapter 21: Blue Rose

I woke up this morning excited like a kid on Christmas morning. I went to work happy that for the next few days I would be enjoying time with my girls, something that is much needed. I can finally catch up with them sharing all the new things that have been going on in my life. It's just not the same talking over the phone. Work was surprisingly smooth; Lisa was still trying to stay in my good graces, so she was overly nice, insisting to finish a report that I was working on. If I had not finished already, I would have probably taken her up on that offer. I didn't have a long shift today because I wanted to make sure that I made it to the airport in time for my flight. I had no intention of going home after work, so I packed my things last night and put them in my car. As I was preparing to take a short break, I called Mrs. Thompson who let me know that things were going great as Mr. Thompson had been discharged resting comfortably at home. That made me feel at ease leaving knowing that they had made it home.

On my way to grab some lunch, I was in such a good mood that I gave Naeem a call who answered seemingly surprised to have received my call. We talked for a short period when I asked him to meet for lunch not sure if he would take me up on the offer being that it is the middle of a workday, but he did. We met at this sub shop not too far from my job. He walked in looking as if he works out daily wearing gray slacks and plaid blue- and white-collar shirt holding a bouquet of blue roses. I had never had blue roses, but they were beautiful. He asked, "do you know the meaning behind blue roses?" "Not knowing that roses, any flowers for that matter had meanings so I asked. "I can't say that I do. Enlighten me." "Well, they can symbolize mystery or attaining the impossible." "Interesting, so what enticed you to gift these to me if you don't mind me asking." "I was thinking that I'd like to the opportunity to discover the mysteries of Shynelle in the sense of learning what motivates her to wake up every morning to start her day. What makes her smile, what does she enjoy doing in her spare time. Things of that sort and being that you didn't give me a call when I first gave you my number seems to be impossible to achieve so I thought these flowers were perfect." Smiling with flattery that he really made that up on the spot. "Oh really" "Yeah, well I thought that were beautiful like you, so I picked them up on my way but because I was so enthused with having never seen blue roses before I looked them up and that's what I learned. But wait here me out, that doesn't take away the fact that I truly do aspire to attain the impossible with you." He said with a beautiful smile on his face. We continued to talk as we finished up our lunch. I really was enjoying myself, but I had a conference call to get back in time for and he too had to meet with some clients. We hugged as he gave me safe travel instructions hoping to see me once I returned home. I didn't give him a definite yes, but I wasn't opposed. He was intriguing not to mention a true gentleman. Our conversations took me on an emotional high. We could discuss life, travel, fitness, relationships, work, and each topic with him were very insightful. With him things were different, it was like I was hanging with a friend who I genuinely enjoyed spending time with desiring to learn more about him at a slow pace that was perfect for me. It may seem crazy, but it was the simplicity in the things that we did that allowed me to see pass the over-the-top gestures to pure beauty of a man that he is displaying at the time. I made it back to work with a few minutes to prepare for my conference call. When Lisa and I finished the conference call Lisa asked, "That smiles must mean that you and Ken made up?" I hope so." I didn't respond I just smiled grabbing my things as I exited the conference room. She didn't try her usual pushy antics surprisingly which was really pleasing. I went to my office to finish up my day.

Unfortunately, I forgot my dress at home which resulted in me having to make quick stop. Luckily, I planned my time out perfectly in the event something like this were to happen. When I arrived, I grabbed my dress then routed immediately back to the car. By the time I approached my car I received a call from Ken who now seems apologetic for his behavior stating that communication when he is upset has always been a character flaw. I too apologized but because I was in a hurry, I cut the call short. He requested that we speak later tonight so I let him know if I had time that I would give him a call. I didn't know how to feel. I let Ken know that we would be exclusive as we were dating getting to no one another and I meant that, but it has been a week since the incident. When I tried to discuss things with him, he neglected to reply. It wasn't until his uncle got sick that he reached out to me. I was under the impression that he and I were over. Honestly, I thought I would be a little bit more hurt, but I just didn't want to ruin the relationship that I have built with Mr. and Mrs. Thompson, they mean a lot to me. I guess it bothers me so because I am big on communication as it helps to elevate unnecessary stress which can just be resolved through talking. I really felt as though I was falling for him, he did most of the right things, made time for me as much as possible even helped me reach out to my estranged mother. I didn't know what to do, I just didn't have the answer to this one so I will table that until later.

When I arrived at the airport I didn't have to wait for a shuttle as there was one pulling up as I got there. I sat at the front getting to my destination within five minutes. When I got inside the airport, I checked in easily, got to my terminal and it was time to board. I had a row all to myself. I was able to just relax enjoying the beauty of the flight. When I arrived at my connecting flight, I had an hour to spare. My father reached out letting me know that they had landed informing me that the parents will be going to a jazz club later tonight so if he doesn't see me today that he will be joining us for breakfast in the morning. I sent him a text confirming to make time for him tomorrow. I sat waiting for my flight while listening to music when a lady got on the intercom stating that due the storm the flight to Miami would be delayed. I was just hoping that I made it in time to make it to hang with everyone. I have been looking forward to this for a while. As I was sitting there a video comes through from Vanessa of everyone having a great time at the bar. They were doing karaoke, something I loved although it's one thing that people least expect about me. It made me a little bit irritated that the flight was delayed; however, I didn't want to fly in that rain. I was glad when the other flight landed because at the end of my last flight is when it started to thunder, freaking me out. But before I could get too anxious the pilot landed the plane.

After the initial hour it appeared that we would be waiting for a while, so I decided to get some food. I went to the nearest restaurant so that I could keep my terminal in view just in case they decided make a move. I sat and ordered a salmon salad with a bottle of water. As I waited, I watched a movie on my iPad. It kept me occupied until my food came that I regret purchasing. It didn't have any flavor whatsoever; I mean not even the salad dressing helped. I pushed my plate to the side, paid for my meal then headed back to my terminal when I received a text from Naeem asking if I had made it to my destination. I replied letting him know that I had a delay. He gave me a call on his way home to help me pass time, so he says but I didn't mind I was glad that he called. He let me know that he had a game this weekend as he created a flag football team at his company for those who still liked sports a way to stay fit while enjoying the game of football. We talked for about thirty minutes when I thought I heard them say my flight was preparing to board, so I ended the call abruptly. However, when I arrived at my terminal it was a false alarm, deciding to just take a seat. I wanted to call Naeem back, but I decided to wait. I had the urge to explain to him why I didn't call him when he initially gave me his number, but I didn't want to make things awkward. I had a lot of things to think about, but I really needed some guidance because this is something that I have no experience in, dating is just not something that I know much about admittedly. I continued to wait while I finished up the book that I started a little while ago pleased with the ending. I searched to see if there was a sequel and to my surprise there was, so I ordered it and it should arrive after my trip. I waited for over three hours when I finally fell asleep. By the time I woke up we were still waiting so I went to the restroom then ventured off to find something to eat this time looking over the menu before deciding. I found a sushi spot, so I gave it a try. Pleased with my decision, I enjoyed my dinner. I gave Yazmine a call who appeared to be having a great time. She was upset that I wouldn't make it in time for tonight, but she left a key for me to get in the house just in case it was late, and they were already gone. I didn't book a hotel this time because I had no intention of staying in one. I knew that Yazmine would have the guest room nice and clean for me just the way I like it, not having to guess if the sheets are clean. We ended the call so that she could get back to her guest and I finished up my dinner. I watched the game highlights that they had on the tv. Finally, I finished deciding to walk around but there was only so much to do in an airport. I refused to spend any more money on the overpriced items here, I mean for food alone cost a fortune. I decided to walk the length of the side of the terminal I was on just to get some exercise in and to pass time. I walked for an hour probably looking like a wierdo to the people that saw me walking back and forth but I didn't care. When I finished, I decided to ask the lady at the desk how long is the wait now. She explained that it should be within the next hour, so I decided to take a seat continue waiting as if I had any other option. Vanessa and Yazmine continued to send me pictures texting me which made me happy, but I would have rather been with them making the memories but sometimes things are just out of my control, which makes it easier for me to just go with the flow. It was midnight when it was time to finally board the plane. Everyone was tired, annoyed, and just ready to get to their destinations. This flight was a little shorter, so I didn't plan on sleeping but when I had the row to myself, I nodded off quickly.

Once I arrived at my destination, I was drained. Yazmine arranged for me to have a car pick me up so after the hassle of finding my luggage I headed to my car. The traffic leaving the airport was ridiculous especially being since it was late at night. Once I arrived at Yazmine's house, they had been gone for about an hour by now. I ate the plate of food that she left out for me because I was hungry even though it was too late to be eating, I had every intention to work it off in the morning. Once I finished, I went to the guest room that Yazmine had decked out for me. It was so refreshing, she even put some fresh flowers in there for me. I put my things away, got in the shower and flopped on the bed cutting on the tv. I browsed for a while when I received a text. I couldn't find my phone, but I could hear it. After flipping the room upside down, I found it underneath the blanket. Thinking that it had to be either

Yazmine or Vanessa sending more pictures to my surprise it was Naeem. The text message read "I hadn't heard from you since you had to get off the phone for your flight in a hurry. I pray you made it safely and have a great time with your friends. I hope to see you when you return." With all that has been going on today, I forgot to let him know that I made it, so I sent him a message letting him know that I made it asking if he were up. He responded letting me know that he was up watching a movie, so I gave him a call. He answered and before I knew it, we were on the phone watching the movie together.

When the movie went off, we talked for another hour until I began to nod. I could also tell that he was getting tired, so I ended the call. Before I was ready to lay down, I got up to get a glass of water. I found my favorite slippers, put on my robe, and went towards the kitchen. Unlike my two-bedroom condominium, Yazmine's house was huge. Although she left a light on for me it was still dark in here, so I found myself using my phone light to guide me down the hall. I was searching trying to find a light switch, but I couldn't find one when I finally made it to the kitchen. I hurried to find a glass to get some water so that I could hurry back to my room. I was hoping that they hurry up to get home soon. I finally found a glass, as I was walking towards the refrigerator, I heard a noise, paranoid I started to look around, but I didn't see anything. I continued to the refrigerator, but I heard the noise again but this time it was louder but because it was so damn dark in the house I couldn't see much past the kitchen. I tried not frightening myself too much, so I got my water drank it but as I was putting my glass in the sink, I heard footsteps. Before I knew it, I was running down the hallway bumping my toe on the panel of the doorway. Once I made it to my room, I locked the door trying to figure out how to open the fancy ass window. My heart was racing but I couldn't get the window open, so I went to the bathroom.

I was in the bathroom for fifteen minutes, but I didn't hear anything else. When I attempted to call Yazmine, I realized that I didn't have my phone. I had no intentions of leaving the bathroom, but I didn't want to sit in there all night. As I was sitting there contemplating on my next move, I heard a noise again, this time it was outside my room. I felt my heart drop in panic as I wished that I had just gotten dressed to meet them out tonight. That's when I saw a silver metal bat sitting in the corner. I got up, grabbed it, and stood ready to beat the shit out of whatever was on the other side of the door.

Chapter 22: Bat & Slippers

Today has been anything short of amazing. After karaoke, Bryson and I had some fun together then we went over to Mason house. We played video games for a few hours then it was time to get ready for tonight. I was upset that Shynelle flight was delayed but she was super chill about the situation as always. I hadn't had the opportunity to talk to Terrance about his job offer due to our schedules. I got slammed with training and he was busy working on a project. When I approached him about it this morning, he asked that I save it until after the grand opening so that we could just enjoy our time with everyone unlike last time. I agreed so we decided to have the conversation later. I dropped Bryson off at the hotel stopping by my parents' room to give my mom a top as she got a makeup stain on hers. After I helped her get sexy for their date night, I checked in on Vanessa who was hanging out with her new younger sister who fits in perfectly with us. After I left the hotel, I went home so that I could change for the night. I was met by Mason who brought a few drinks. When I walked into the room Terrance was finishing up getting dressed so I took over the bathroom with my things. An hour later I was dressed, ready to start the night. Vanessa and

Bryson were now here in the kitchen taking shots with Mason and Terrance. I came in with them handing me my cup. Once we finished our ride pulled up to take us to this club. When we arrived at the club the line was ridiculous, but Mason had connection because we bypassed the line entering the club with no issues. Bryson childish as can be hyped his younger brother up who was just always so chill about everything. When we got into the club, we were escorted to our booth, when I say Mason truly has come into town and made a name for himself along with him having his social media platform.

Once they stopped playing the techno music, playing some hip-hop Vanessa and I got up to dance. She and I know how to put on a show. We danced all night. Terrance and Bryson chilled in the booth most of the night getting up when the DJ played certain songs saying the words nothing major. It was lit for sure. I was enjoying myself, but I had so many nerves with excitement about the soft opening for the family tomorrow evening that I was ready to go. Vanessa, who was having a little too much fun needed to go. Bryson, Terrance, and Mason were still having a good time so I told them that I would get us home. Because they didn't want us to leave alone, Terrance left with us. Vanessa was in no condition to be alone, so we took her to our house. On the ride home, Vanessa threw up all over the Uber driver car which meant we had to pay a cleaning fee plus leave a good tip. But what made it so bad was afterwards she asked the man to cut the music up because it was too quiet in the car. Terrance and I trying hard not to laugh as the driver, an older gentleman with a pissed looked on his face, held his composure not to kick her out of his vehicle.

When we pulled up to our destination Terrance handed the driver another tip causing him to smile extremely hard, so I asked, "how much did you give him?" "One hundred, for dealing with Vanessa wild self." We both laughed as we walked in the house. We forgot to cut the lights on before we left so it was difficult trying to maneuver through a dark house trying to help my friend walk. When we finally get into the house Vanessa falls on the floor so I let Terrance try to help her up when she said, "if yall cut on the damn lights, I could walk through this maze myself." Everyone trying to laugh quietly not to wake Shynelle. Vanessa, who has regurgitated everything that she has eaten on the Ubers back seat now seems to feel better as Terrance helps her into the house. As we were approaching the kitchen, I could hear that the someone was in there, so I walked that way. By the time I made it there it was empty, so I guess I was just hearing things. I didn't want to wake Shynelle, so I helped Vanessa get situated on the other side of the house in our additional guest room. After getting her together I met back up with Terrance who was standing at the kitchen counter eating cold wings. "Baby, these wings hit different when you are drunk. You want one?" I shake my head at him as I take the wing out of his hand. When we were finished, we tried to creep pass Shynelle room, but I noticed that her light was on so as Terrance went on to the room I stopped. I grabbed the door, but it was locked. I was going to leave but I could see her shadow, I knocked. When she didn't say anything, I realized that she must be scared so not to freak her out more than she probably already was I say in a soft tone, "you scary slut, it's just me Yazmine" as I laughed at her on the other side of the door. When she opens the door, I see before me this crazy woman wearing a yellow bath robe, big ass slippers holding a baseball bat. Laughing hysterically at her Terrance walks pass stops looks at her, shakes his head and continues to the kitchen again. "Yazmine, it is not funny, this house is huge, and you don't believe in cutting lights on apparently." After I gather myself from laughing, I finally respond, "Shynelle, honestly what were you about to do with that bat?" "Girl, I was about to beat your ass." We both laughed as she put the bat down to give me a hug. I explained to her that Vanessa got sick, so we came home early. We sat up talking for an hour, but I could tell that she was tired, so I let her get some rest. When I walked in my room, I saw Terrance laid out across the bed in nothing but his boxers and socks. I covered him up with a blanket then took a shower.

The next morning, I woke up as Shynelle was preparing for a run on the beach. I was going to join her, but I wanted to straighten up for the chef this morning. I hired the young lady that is Mason's sous chef to cater brunch this morning so that Mason could have the opportunity to sleep in and enjoy time with the family as well. As I was finishing up the cleaning the chef arrived. I let her in giving her a tour of the kitchen informing her where everything is so that I could get dressed for the day. I went to check on Vanessa who was still sound asleep. When I walked in the room Terrance was just getting out the shower.

When I finished getting dressed, the aroma from the kitchen just justified that I made the right decision with hiring her for the restaurant. When I walked in the kitchen, she had everything looking and smelling phenomenal. I was pleased with her presentation. I cut on the music as guest were starting to arrive. Mason had made it as he and the chef were in the kitchen talking about tonight. My parents were out on the deck with Ms. Gyles, her husband, and his daughter. Bryson was in the front with Terrance talking sports. Vanessa was getting dressed as Bryson had to bring her clothes. Shynelle was directing her father on how to get my house. The morning was going well. I had everything in place for tonight which wasn't going to be much; however, it will allow the opportunity for feedback from family members who don't mind telling the truth which is what we want to better the outcome for tomorrow. I was excited even though I still needed to talk to Terrance about the moving situation. Once everyone had arrived the music was turned up a little louder which resulted in Ms. Gyles giving dance lessons. By the second song all the ladies were on the dance floor dancing, having a good time. I didn't want it to be too formal so I had things set up buffet style so that the chef could mingle enjoying herself as well. It was such a good vibe.

Chapter 23: Red Flags

Enjoying myself on the dance floor, Yazmine tells everyone that the food is prepared so we could eat. I fixed my plate then joined my dad at the table on the deck as his wife was catching up with the other moms, still dancing while talking. "Hi dad, I am so glad to see you." "Likewise baby girl. So, tell me how have things been going for you?" "Things have been going great actually?" "I love to hear that, so how are things with that Ken fella? Is he still treating my baby girl well? And when am I going to meet him or is it still not that serious?" I have never introduced anyone to my father because for one I haven't dated and two you must really mean something to me to meet my parents. "Well, may I ask you a question?" "Of course," "Ken and I had a miscommunication but, in that timeframe, I realized that I have never dated. I was infatuated with a fairytale because I never thought that I deserved it, then comes along this man who opens my eyes to that possibility. Now, I feel that I deserve it but not sure if I want it with him. I believe he is a great guy but maybe he isn't my person. You know what mom is for you. I don't know dad maybe I am just overthinking things as usual. I don't want to make a mistake." "Well, baby girl only you can decide but maybe you are right. He may just be that fella to open your eyes to new possibilities even if it's not with him. I am true believer that things happen for a reason. Just think on it and do what is best for you, trust your gut. I know that whatever you decide will be the best decision." I sat there finishing up brunch as I continued to talk with my dad. His wife who was finally done dancing came to join us showing me pictures of the house that they have renovated.

Later that day, Vanessa and I cleaned up so that Yazmine could prepare for the restaurant soft opening tonight. After we finished, everyone decided to leave heading back to their hotels so that they could also prepare for tonight. Yazmine didn't want me to help tonight because she wanted me to enjoy myself along with everyone else, so she told me to stay then come to the restaurant at the allotted time. I didn't have much to do being that I had taken my run this morning. I was still pondering on the conversation that I had with my father knowing what I wanted to do. So, I called Ken who didn't answer. I didn't bother to leave him a message I decided that I would talk with him whenever he returns my call.

Later that evening I showered, preparing for the night. When I was dressed, Terrance came back to pick me up to go to the soft opening. When we pulled up, she had redone the signage which was appealing, an eye catcher. When I walked in, I was blown away with how amazing it looked in there. Everything was beautiful. Within twenty minutes, everyone had finally arrived, so they began to bring the food.

Everything was great, it was as if each dish evolved into something better making me anticipate the next menu item. We hadn't seen Mason the entire night as he was in the kitchen creating magic, but as he was coming to make his appearances the waitress was taking our order to determine which of the two dessert items. There were only two options for the night, blueberry shortcake or the crème brule. I leaned over to Vanessa who had become very quiet once the food started to arrive. At this point she appeared flushed, so I asked, "is everything alright?" "I don't what happened, but I don't feel well. We are waiting for Mason so that Bryson can take me to the hotel. I don't want to get anyone else sick." "Okay, well I will let me know if you need anything. Try to get some rest. Hopefully it doesn't last long so that you can join us tomorrow." "I hope so, I really…" Before she could finish her statement, she ran off to the bathroom, so I went after her to make sure she was okay. After helping her as she puked up everything she had consumed in the past week, I helped her clean up then walked her to the car where we were met by Bryson. Yazmine had been going back and forth between us and the kitchen as the small number of staff she had working truly kept her moving tonight. She loves it, she loves to be busy no matter what we say to her it's just her thing. With all that was going on I missed dessert, so the waitress had it nicely presented in a to go container on the table. We left the waitress a nice tip she was truly exceptional for it being her first time ever hosting.

We were supposed to be out of here by nine tonight but when our families link up it's hard to separate them. So here it is eleven pm leaving the restaurant, the staff however had already been long gone. Once at Yazmine house we threw on some cozy pajamas and hung out in my room because I convinced her to watch scary movies with me. Within ten minutes we were both on the bed sleep. When I woke up Yazmine was up as usual preparing for the day. Vanessa and I wanted to surprise Yazmine with hair and make-up, but I wasn't sure if Vanessa was feeling up to it this morning, so I called to check on her. When she answered she was back to her perky, vibrant self again. She let me know that she would be pulling up shortly. I walked in on Yazmine who was laying out her outfit for the night. Before I could look at it, the doorbell rang so I went to answer the door. It was Vanessa along with the make-up artist and stylist. Mason got us their information from their photoshoot so we knew that she would like their work. She was happy for her surprise even though she didn't show it much we could tell that she was very appreciative. We all got pampered taking turns either getting our hair or make up done. Yazmine was finished first, so she hurried to get dress. As we were finishing up, she walked back in the room wearing black high rise wide leg dress pants, long sleeve studded mesh inserts v-neck top, and the cutest back heels which looked amazing on her. "You're beautiful Yazmine" I said to her as she seemed to be second guessing her choice of outfit now. Vanessa screamed, "Girl yes! It's sexy but not too much. It's giving I am a businesswoman, but I can look good doing so, very much says this is my shit. You have arrived at my grand opening!" As she jumped up looking crazy with her hair half curled, make up almost done looking a bit crazy dancing with Yazmine who now seemed a bit surer of herself. I popped open a bottle of champagne giving a toast to my friend who took a risk, saw in through good bad and indifferent in hopes to create family legacy alongside her younger brother. It was so heartfelt that she almost let a tear out. We all hugged, did a little dance as we cheered her off.

Vanessa and I were finally dressed, preparing to leave for the restaurant. When we pulled up there was a line around the corner of people waiting to get in as there was still an hour before opening. When Vanessa and I walked in everything was polished, ready for the night. Yazmine was giving her staff a pep talk getting everyone to know their roles for tonight. Our families were already there sitting in a private section of the restaurant so that we would be out of the way of the actual crowd. Her parents were so proud that they were taking several pictures. I believe Mason had to ask them kindly to get out of the kitchen area at one point. As time was nearing opening, we walked to the front with Yazmine who stopped midway clasping her hands over her mouth in awe of the turnout. She tried hard not to cry but Mason grabbed her giving her a hug whispering in her ear, "sis, thank you for this opportunity." She had the most contented smile on her face as she patted the tear from her cheek. Vanessa went over to help her make sure her make up wasn't messed up. Then the entire family cheered as she and Mason on as we walked to the door preparing to open. We watched Yazmine and Mason thank everyone for coming out then opened the doors. Within ten minutes the place was packed to capacity with still a line of people still waiting to get in. It was busy but she had groomed her staff well because things were running smoothly. She was back in her groove of working, walking around helping staff, speaking with guest. It was truly a pleasure to be a part of this day with her.

I was sitting enjoying a drink when I received a call from Ken. I wasn't in the mood for speaking with him, so I ignored it, but he called back two more times. I put my phone in my purse went over to Bryson to catch up with him. During our conversation I hear, "so here you go entertaining yet another gentleman, Shynelle." I looked up to Ken standing in front of me speaking extremely crazy when Bryson asked if everything is okay as he began to stand up. That is when I also saw Terrance get up from the table to walk over. I stopped them letting them know that I had everything under control pulling Ken to the side. "Ken, what are you doing here?" "I came to surprise you so that we could talk but I see you already brought a date. I guess you're just another not going to call you the word, but you know what you are." I see my dad stand up before he could finish his statement. I was looking at this guy in utter disgust with the awful nonfactual words that he regurgitated about me was an extreme low. My dad at this point had gotten up from his seat now standing beside me as I requested that he leaves. He refused but when Terrance and Bryson walked back over, he threw the flowers at my feet walking away. My emotions were in a state of disarray from Ken's behavior. I felt uneasy that this man who has been such a gentleman displaying such undesirable behavior and opinions of me. I tried to go on with my night but in the back of my mind his words were on repeat. I remember in one of my conversations with Mrs. Thomas stating that Ken was truly a good guy, but he still had some issues to overcome. She never really spoke anything else on it just let me know to take my time with him. I didn't think much of it but reflecting thinking of her soft frail hands holding mine as she spoke those words staring into my eyes. Not to mention what she said to me the other day, it made me think that she was trying to tell me that he could do something like this. I already planned to end ties with him, but this solidifies my decision for sure. In the mist of me analyzing the situation Yazmine who must have heard what happened came over to make sure I was okay. "Shy, he must not know I'll kick his ass over you. He doesn't know you mine." as she pinched my cheek giving me a hug. She knew just what to say to make me smile and to get out of my head.

Later that evening after leaving the restaurant, everyone went off on their own day adventures. Terrance decided to stay at the restaurant all day with his wife so I tagged along with Bryson and Vanessa who thought it would be fun to go to the amusement park. I wasn't into paying to ride a ride that would scare me shitless, but I went with them anyways. It turned out to be fun, I even got on a few of the not so over the top rides. As we were hanging out, I received a text from Naeem stating "I hope you are enjoying yourself. I just thought of you, so I wanted to say hi-Naeem" I was a little on the edge being that Ken had just shown me his erratic behavior that I wasn't sure if I wanted to even date anyone. I was sitting on the bench reading the message as Vanessa came to sit beside me after buying a bottle of water. "Shy, you know you can't stop dating just because one guy showed you, he wasn't shit." I looked at her in shock because it was as if she were sitting in my head reading my thoughts. "What if he is just the same Vanessa?" "Well, if you stop talking to him, how will you know? I mean if you based your opinions of everyone just on one person than you will never have a partner. I mean shit, you just started dating, take a chance and see how it goes. Ken was just not your guy and that is okay. You know how many Kens I have met in my dating life?" I sat there letting her words sink in when Bryson grabbed us to get on another ride. When we made it to his suggested ride, I sat there holding our bags because there was just no way that I was getting on a ride that looked as though it would throw me off. They were insane for getting on it.

When we left the amusement park it was late; we were tired and drained but because we all leave tomorrow, we were hanging out with Yazmine and Mason tonight. They arrived at Yazmine's house just as we were pulling up both looking as they didn't have any energy left. We all made it to the living room where everyone was laid out. It was evident that no one had any energy from our long days, so we voted on a movie to watch. It was the perfect chill night before leaving back to our busy lives. The next morning Vanessa and Bryson left to the airport as they checked out of their hotel yesterday, staying the night here so they could leave early in the morning. Mason went home to prepare for work today. Yazmine was up working as usual, and Terrance cheerfully headed off to work. I was packing my things so that I could leave to the airport, hoping that my flight is better than the one coming here. When I was finished Yazmine grabbed her things so that she could take me to the airport on her way to work. I could tell that she had something on her mind, so I asked, "what has you so quiet this morning?" "Shy, Terrance wants us to move again. I was considering it because he is my husband, and it would be very close to you but after yesterday I don't think I can. I am finally in a happy place; I have things going great for me and shit look at me I am taking care of myself again. I just don't want the stress of starting over again. Not to mention how happy Mason was yesterday made all this worth it. So, my dilemma is how do I communicate that to my husband without him feeling as I don't support him?" I was stomped for words because I didn't want to give her advice on something that I had no knowledge on. "I don't know what to say Yazmine because I don't want to give you the wrong advice. I just think you could share those same feelings you shared with me to him. I am certain you two will figure this out, you always do." "I hope so. Oh, and Vanessa shared with me you not wanting to date because of Ken. Well, here is my unsolicited advice. Fuck him! Go on a date with Naeem. Give the guy a chance, let him reveal himself to you but don't assume that he will be a jerk just because Ken was. I want to see you happy Shy, but you can't continue to run away from things at the first sign of fear. You will miss out on life in doing that. Okay, now think about that on your flight and give me a hug. I am going to miss your scary ass." We hug before I get out to walk into the airport. No matter how many times we do this, it is always sad when we leave each other.

When I arrived home, I put my things away then looked for something to eat. I couldn't find anything that I wanted so I decided to treat myself to lunch. I was still wearing my airport attire that was because it was so comfortable that I didn't want to change. So, I decided not to. I had been thinking about what Vanessa and Yazmine said to me, so I decided to listen to them. I hadn't responded to Naeem since he sent the text on yesterday. I am not sure if he will even answer when I call but I decide to give it a try. On the third ring, I was preparing to hang up when I heard him say, "hello". I talked to him apologizing about yesterday with him being very understanding. "Naeem, I am not dolled up in anything fancy, but would you like to hang with me today? I was thinking of grabbing a bite to eat." "You called at the perfect time; I was just heading to the bar to watch the game. I would love for you to join me." I took him up on the offer. I was nervous but I wanted to take everyone advice not giving up on this dating things because although I ignored the red flags with Ken doesn't mean Naeem will turn out to be the same. It still lingered in my mind how things will turn out between the Thomas's. It's a lot to fathom but in the end, it was time to focus on me as I have shown up for everyone else; it's time to show up for me for a change.

When I arrived at the bar, he was sitting there waiting for me. I approached him as he embraced me with the gentlest hug. He was giving me the highlights of the game when I interrupted him saying, "I didn't call you when we first met because I was kind of dating someone else. It, however, is over now all a crazy situation but I wanted to be upfront with you so you could make the decision as to if you want to continue to talk to me. I really like you and would love to continue to get to know you, but I just wanted to be open and honest with you." He sits there with a smile on his face. "I guess those blue roses gave me luck. Thank you for your honesty, not many people have that trait, so I appreciate it. I would also love to continue to get to know you as well. Believe me when I say, dating is new to me too, I haven't dated since my divorce so let's take all the time, we need to get to know one another and enjoy this game cause my team about to get this WIN!" I laugh as he yelled high fiving the bartender who must also be a fan of the team. We ordered wings and a beer as we watched the game. With him it doesn't feel like a date, just two friends hanging out having a good time. I wasn't sure what to think of it just now, but I am glad I didn't deny myself the opportunity of finding out what it could become.

Chapter 24: Back Flips

My trip to Yazmine's grand opening was everything that I hoped for and more even with the minor hiccups. Bryson and I jokingly played around with the idea that I was pregnant but when we thought about it there was a strong possibility that it could be true. We frightened ourselves so much that to put it to rest, in our hotel room we took a test that came back negative. Although we desire to start a family someday, we want to take things slow to acquire a knowledge of one another outside of the friendship we have built, which is why we have decided to move in together. At first, I was hesitant because I have never lived with anyone besides my mom, not even a roommate, so this is going to be an adjustment for me. However, this allows me the opportunity to be present, forcing me to deal with things head on instead of running home when things are too much to deal with as my counselor would say. We also discussed using the money I pay for my place to put into a saving to go towards our new home that we are planning to start building soon.

When we made it from the airport, we planned to use today to move my things out. Bryson went to get a U-Haul while I finished packing.

When I walked into my apartment there was a feeling of sadness that charged through my body as I looked around my apartment that was now filled with boxes. Although this is a change that I know that I am ready to embark upon, it doesn't diminish the fact that change is scary. I put my bags down walking around my place looking at everything reminiscing of all the great memories that I created while living in this place. I could now see the slight dent on the wall that I had hide behind a mirror resulting from Yazmine wanting to prove that she could do a back flip. Then there is the scuff on the kitchen floor where Shynelle fell while playing adult trap musical chairs on one of our game nights. I have so many significant memories here but like my friends who have moved on starting new chapters in their lives, it was now my turn. Although nerves are kicking my ass, I am excited to see where this life changing experience takes me.

After hours of loading the truck, putting my furniture in storage, and taking my other items to my new home, I was finally done. I didn't have to turn my key in until tomorrow, but I did my final walk through ensuring that it was spotless. Once I made it back in the living room, it was evident that I was saying goodbye to a piece of me. I was starting to question if I were making the right decision when Bryson came over, grabbed my hand, saying, "this is where you say goodbye to Ms. Vanessa and say hello to Mrs. Vanessa." It was then when I realized that change is inevitable towards progression accepting that this decision is helping me become the woman I desire to be. Besides, I still have an extra room over there just in case he gets on my nerves, and I need to get away, baby steps.

Chapter 25: Hurdles

I am still in disbelief that the opening exceeded my expectations. It was yesterday that I came to the realization that I have been so invested in this place because of my aspirations of wanting to create family legacy. In the process, I fell in love with being able to provide a place of work to those who are trying to figure things out. There were so many staff members who came up to me since working expressing how this job opportunity is helping them to fund their dreams with me being able to work with their school schedule. Nyla, who I have always been drawn to came to me crying yesterday thanking me for believing in her enough to give her this opportunity. Then there is the piece of wanting to create a family legacy. When Mason hugged me right before we opened, it made every stressful encounter since opening this place well worth it. I couldn't do this for my parents as I initially wanted but I created a platform for my brother who has been nothing but appreciative yet supportive that I couldn't help but breakdown on yesterday. I knew someone was going to try to get proof of me crying and that damn slut Vanessa was the one. As she walked over to help me, she snuck a picture that she sent to me this morning as they were boarding the flight, she is lucky I didn't see if before she left. Overall, this feeling is something that I have been longing for my entire life not being able to really communicate it before but now I am certain this is it. I still want to keep my rental properties back home, but this is something that I really have grown to love which makes it even harder for me to tell Terrance that I can't go with him. I just hopes he supports my decision just as I have supported him. He and I have plans to talk this evening to discuss everything since we have made it through the biggest hurdle. Shynelle let me know that her flight was preparing to take off as I was up the street from work. When I arrived, there were a few people standing in line but didn't compare at all to yesterday. When I walked in Mason was talking to his staff giving them directive for today. Nyla was ensuring that staff were clocking in, giving them their roles for today. When I walked into my office there were so many flowers from family, Terrance, and friends congratulating me. I was in awe of the support. We had twenty minutes before opening so I did my walk through. The inventory had been updated since yesterday, order form has been completed for needed supply, the restaurant looked magnificent, and Mason was preparing to start his amazing food. I went to the front to help the host at the front door. There still weren't many people outside just a few more from when I arrived but I still stayed upfront. Things were going smoothly; staff were very attentive to the customers, and we were receiving great reviews. I decided to walk back to my office to submit the order for the items that we needed. I was in my office for about twenty minutes when I looked on the camera seeing that we now have a packed restaurant. It was as if everyone in the area decided to come here for their lunch break. When I walked out to greet the customers to see how they were enjoying their meals. There was this one gentleman who was so excited that he finally found his new favorite restaurant. I went to the kitchen to see how things were going and Mason had things under control.

On my break, I had three messages. One from Terrance saying that he would like to take me out for dinner tonight. The second message was from Shynelle letting me know that she was meeting with Naeem, that she will call me later to let me know how it goes. Then there was a damn text message from Vanessa of the dent I put in her wall years ago. I don't know why they tried to play me; I did the damn flip the wall just got in my way. I responded to everyone then continued my walk just enjoying the feeling that I had right now. I was getting more anxious the later it got in the day in anticipation of talking to Terrance about my decision. What if he decides that he still wants to leave, how would we work? What if he gets upset with me deciding to want nothing more to do with me? What if he stays but never gets this opportunity again then resents me? I have so many scenarios running rapid in my brain that I had to take a moment to just breathe. I wasn't sure of the outcome, but I knew my stance and I am prepared for the outcome of my decision.

Later that evening, as it was nearing the time for me to leave, I grab my things to go. Terrance gave me a call letting me know that he was on his way. As I was getting closer to my destination my heart began to race. I was beginning to panic. When I walked in, I see Terrance smiling as if he is about to hear me say that I am ready to take on Arizona with him. I hope he can forgive me. I sit down to join him engaging in the small talk of how my day was and so on. By the time we got our food my hands were so sweaty as if I had placed them in a pale of water, but I don't think Terrance noticed. It was then I heard those words, "so Yazmine, you have had plenty of time to think. What did you decide?" I stare across the table at this man that I love who has been working for this type of opportunity since I met him preparing to tell him that I can't go with him right now. "Terrance, I have had time to think and…." I was fortunate to be interrupted by the server bringing the rest of our food. When she walked away Terrance began to eat so I tried to pretend as though we were not in the middle of a serious conversation, but he hadn't. "So, you were saying?" Before I knew it, I blurted out, "I can't go with you to Arizona, Terrance." He looks up from eating his food and that smile that he just had was gone. He appeared sadden, hurt, and confused. "So, what are you saying?" "I am saying I can't go with you, maybe we can try long distance for a while to see how things go here for me. Baby I just can't leave right now, with all that I have worked so hard for. And I know that you really want this job, so I support your decision I just can't go with you." He looks at me still with this hurt look on his face. Dinner was quiet for the next twenty minutes, but I just couldn't take it anymore, so I said, "so what do you think?" "I think that my wife is telling me that she doesn't want to go with me, and I don't know how to feel about that. However, I understand why…" The waiter came again interrupting us, but I wanted him to continue so once the waiter left, I gave him the look to finish. "I understand why you don't want to go which is why I turned down the position." I looked over at him still hurt because I didn't want him to resent his decision later. "I am sorry Terrance." He didn't say anything for a minute which felt like an eternity. "You don't have to be Yazmine I felt like it was my turn to support your dream." I smiled then he continues on, "Yeah, well when I declined the position last week, later that afternoon I was approached saying that they had offered the opportunity to someone else but get this; the chef executive that I have been working with since being here is retiring this month and he has offered me his position same benefits, perks, and opportunity here baby. We both get to do what we love." I smile throwing a dinner roll at him. "Congratulation's jerk! You could have opened with that statement." "Fuck no, I like to see the soft side of your tough ass sometimes. You look so cute being sensitive and shit. I love you woman." He says as he perks his lips blowing me a kiss across the table. We laugh enjoying the remaining of our dinner. On my ride home it was apparent I married the perfect asshole.

Reflecting over my journey to get to where I am today it is evident that on the other side of a storm there is sunshine. Even though, I wish there were fewer rain drops I am pleased to say I withstood the storm arriving to the other side. Arriving home, I see my neighbor sitting on his porch in his favorite robe, so I speak. He flicks me off with a smile on his face then waves. I was so exhilarated with joy that Terrance and I were both getting the outcome that we desired I threw one back up at him. I instantly regretted my impulsive reaction that I quickly turned into his driveway, hoping out extremely apologetic. "I am so sorry; I don't know what made me do that to you." "Because I did it to you first, stop apologizing. Have a seat and keep me company for a while." I couldn't turn him down because I was so baffled that I had just flicked this old man off that I had no choice but to sit. He sat staring for a while then finally spoke, "congratulations on your restaurant I hear it was a good turnout. It was on the news." "Thank you, it was. You should stop by sometime on me of course." He smiles then replies, "can't just be giving stuff away, that's not good for business." I sit with my neighbor talking for over an hour mostly me telling him about what has been going on. He listened then suddenly; he jumps up. "You stay put; I will be right back." After a few minutes he walks slowly back out on the porch with an expensive bottle of champagne and the most beautiful champagne flutes. He asks me to open the bottle then pours us each a glass. He passes me my glass then stands holding his glass to make a toast. "Cheers to the success of your restaurant as you prepare to effectively conqueror the hurdles to come. Take it from an old grouch like me because that will not be the last obstacle you will face. Just remember what you learned this go around." I stand to toast with the old grouch who, for once, I agreed with.

Tequila Barksdale's first body of work is Tears of a Masterpiece. She is a master degreed social worker and rising author whose work demonstrates relatable stories through the lens of fictional women characters aimed to uplift and inspire readers to tackle hardship through a solution driven viewpoint.

www.ingramcontent.com/pod-product-compliance
Lightning Source LLC
Chambersburg PA
CBHW071158260626
47162CB00003B/1093